A Candlelight Ecstasy Romance™

HIS EYES REVEALED
A NAKED HUNGER. . . .

Assuming the unfamiliar role of aggressor, Lauren explored his body with her hands, sprinkling kisses on his lips, his eyes, his shoulders, and the hair-rough expanse of his chest. Never before had she felt so free, so uninhibited, her own passion mounting as she saw the effect her lovemaking was having on him. His breathing was ragged as he pulled her at last into a demanding embrace.

"I want you, Lauren. My God, how I want you!"

RESTORING LOVE

Suzanne Sherrill

A CANDLELIGHT ECSTASY ROMANCE™

Published by
Dell Publishing Co., Inc.
1 Dag Hammarskjold Plaza
New York, New York 10017

Dell ® TM 681510, Dell Publishing Co., Inc.

Candlelight Ecstasy Romance™ is a trademark of
Dell Publishing Co., Inc., New York, New York.

ISBN: 0–440–16373–0

Printed in the United States of America
First printing—March 1982

Dear Reader:

In response to your continued enthusiasm for Candlelight Ecstasy Romances™, we are increasing the number of new titles from four to six per month.

We are delighted to present sensuous novels set in America, depicting modern American men and women as they confront the provocative problems of modern relationships.

Throughout the history of the Candlelight line, Dell has tried to maintain a high standard of excellence to give you the finest in reading enjoyment. That is and will remain our most ardent ambition.

Anne Gisonny
Editor
Candlelight Romances

To D.W.,
for believing it could happen

CHAPTER ONE

The voices in Reed Donovan's office could be heard plainly in the waiting room. It was not that the walls of Charleston's City Hall were particularly thin. It had been built in 1801, when walls were thick and buildings were solidly constructed. It was just that on this afternoon the men inside were speaking loudly and angrily. At least one of them was.

"Damn it all, Donovan, I want this taken care of and I want it done now. I've got millions riding on this project and I can't wait forever while the fine city fathers go all sentimental about their blasted waterfront. Now can you do it or not?" the deep, rich masculine voice demanded impatiently.

Lauren Mitchell, her hands twisting nervously in her lap as she waited in the outer office, couldn't hear the planning director's reply. She was sure, though, that Reed Donovan was using all his tact to coax his irate visitor into a more reasonable frame of mind.

Although she'd only met Donovan once, at a zoning meeting where he'd taken on a group of angry neighborhood residents, he'd struck her then as the sort of man who could calmly face an erupting volcano.

This time, however, his soothing words were apparently falling on deaf ears. Lauren heard something crash in the office, followed by a muttered exclamation. Then the door was yanked open. The man standing on the threshold, his back to her, filled the doorway with his powerfully built frame. Well over six feet tall, broad-shouldered, and narrow-hipped, his defiant stance made it plain he was beyond soothing. Something in the way he stood there, his body tensed in anger, radiating male vitality, made Lauren shiver involuntarily.

"Just so we understand each other, Donovan," the man snapped, oblivious to the observers in the waiting room, "I'll tell you one last time. I want this straightened out within the next ten days. No more than that or the project will go elsewhere. I don't need this kind of aggravation."

He slammed the door behind him and strode across the room, ignoring the startled glances of both Lauren and Mrs. Cates, Reed Donovan's long-time secretary, who shook her head in exasperation at the outburst.

"That man," she observed confidentially to Lauren, "is impossible. Every time he's in here I think the walls are going to come tumbling down around us. If you ask me, he ought to just take his office building to some other city instead of trying to put it up here in Charleston. It'll be an outright eyesore. Why, I can't think of anybody who wants it, except a bunch of—"

She was prevented from completing the thought by the ringing of the buzzer on her desk.

"Certainly, Mr. Donovan. I'll send her right in."

She gave Lauren a conspiratorial wink, hoping to wipe away the look of uncertainty she saw on her pretty face. "Don't worry, my dear. You'll do just fine."

Lauren took a deep breath, as though bracing herself. "Thanks," she replied softly, struggling mentally to replace her feelings of insecurity with an aura of confidence as she faced her first job interview in five years.

Subtly looking around the office for some sign of the verbal warfare that had just taken place there, she was relieved to see that there was no trace of it. Reed Donovan, his shirt sleeves rolled up, his tie askew, was standing cheerfully behind his desk waiting for her. In his early fifties, he had the rugged, outdoor look of a man who'd spent the early part of his career in the sun, supervising projects of his own. That background, combined with his imperturbable nature and his genuine love for all that Charleston stood for, made him the ideal planning director.

"Mrs. Mitchell, how are you?" he asked, coming forward to greet her. "It's good to see you again, especially under more pleasant circumstances. I thought your neighbors were going to get out the tar and feathers at that meeting—when was it, a year ago?"

"About that, yes. But you stood up under the

11

pressure quite well," she said, trying to make herself relax and match his friendly tone.

"I'm used to it. It comes with the territory around here. I thought your husband handled himself like a real pro that night as well. He was an articulate spokesman for your cause. How is he?"

"My husband died a few months ago, Mr. Donovan," Lauren said flatly, able at last to keep her voice from quivering from the strain of Doug's accident and the long, torturous weeks when his life had hung in the balance.

For a moment Donovan was taken aback. Doug Mitchell had been so young. This woman sitting here now, looking frightened to death, couldn't be more than twenty-five. Her husband might have been a year or two older. No more. What a tragic waste, he thought.

Aloud he said, "I'm sorry, my dear. I had no idea. Is that why you're thinking of returning to work?"

Lauren nodded, thinking of the mounting bills, the house payments, clothes for Holly. Her five-year-old was growing out of everything, from her T-shirts to her sneakers.

"Why did you apply for this particular job?"

For the first time since she'd entered Reed Donovan's office Lauren felt at ease. Her green eyes sparkled as she began to talk enthusiastically about her desire to be an architect, a desire that had been squelched when she'd married during her sophomore year in college.

"It's the old story. We were very young and didn't have much money. I dropped out of school and went to work as a secretary to help out until Doug graduated. Then, shortly after he finished, I found out I was pregnant and that was that. I just never went back to school.

"I'm hoping now that I'll have the chance to finish, taking classes at night. And in the meantime I can't imagine a better place to be working than the planning department. I could learn so much," she said enthusiastically. "Not that I'm here just to learn." She corrected herself quickly. "I mean I really am a good secretary. I think I could make a contribution."

"I'm sure you can, my dear. Mrs. Cates has already told me that your skills are first-rate and if she approves of you, then I see no reason to prolong this. When can you start?"

Lauren, afraid that she'd be left dangling for a few days at least, was startled by the suddenness of his decision.

"You mean I have the job? Just like that?"

"Just like that," he stated, smiling at the look of relief that spread across Lauren's face, wiping away the lines of worry and tension that were so unnatural in someone her age. Thinking of his own daughters and his grandchildren, he hoped someday soon Lauren Mitchell's fragile features would be rid of the pallor and weariness that were the marks of her recent tragedy.

"By the way, has Mrs. Cates warned you what a madhouse this place can be at times?"

"If that little scene I just witnessed was a sample, I don't need any other warnings," Lauren conceded.

A look of dismay flashed briefly across Reed Donovan's face.

"Oh, you heard that, did you? Well, don't mind Leland Cross too much. He's a very determined young man and he gets a bit impatient when obstacles pop up in his path. Right now he's got a rather big obstacle staring him in the face, and he doesn't like it one bit."

"He shouldn't be taking that out on you, though," Lauren insisted, already adopting a protective attitude toward her new boss.

Donovan shrugged. "Why not? Better he take it out on me than the mayor or the council and have the whole thing splashed all over the front page of the paper. By the way," he added, his tone sobering, "that's one thing I must insist on as long as you're working here. No talking to the press. Refer any inquiries directly to me. There are some journalists in this town who'd just love a little advance warning when there's a battle brewing over something as big as the Cross office tower."

Lauren's expression was puzzled. "I'm afraid I've been a bit out of touch. What is the Cross office tower?"

"Never mind. You'll find out all about it soon enough. Now when can you start? Mrs. Cates wants to get out of here in a couple of weeks. I'd like you to work with her for at least a week or so, learn where she's tucked my most important files and how she gets rid of my nuisance callers—things like that."

"I can be here on Monday, if that's soon enough," she responded eagerly.

"That will be just fine," he said, ushering her to the outer office where Mrs. Cates was waiting anxiously for the verdict. "Well, Elsie, I think we've found a real winner in this young lady. If Leland Cross didn't scare her off with his tantrum, I can't think of anything else that will. Can you?"

"He is the worst of the lot," Mrs. Cates agreed. "Honey, I know you'll like it here. Mr. Donovan's got his little quirks, but I can teach you how to keep him in line in no time."

He threw up his hands in mock surrender. "If you two are going to gang up on me already, I might as well give up now and go back to my office and get some work done. I'll be looking forward to seeing you on Monday, Mrs. Mitchell. That is, if Mrs. Cates doesn't talk you out of coming back with some of her horror stories."

"I doubt she can do that, Mr. Donovan," Lauren said with a smile. "And thank you again for being so kind."

An hour later Lauren had picked Holly up from school and the two of them were settled in the bright, airy kitchen of their small, brick carriage house, sharing an afternoon snack of milk and freshly baked oatmeal cookies filled with raisins, Holly's favorite.

"Mommy, David tried to hold my hand today on the playground. I hit him," she announced proudly.

"You hit him? Why would you do that," Lauren questioned, trying to suppress her desire to giggle. "He was just trying to show you that he likes you."

"But I don't like him," Holly explained patiently.

"Since when don't you like David? He's your best friend. And anyway, you shouldn't hit people. Couldn't you have just told him nicely that he was bothering you and then gone to play with someone else?"

Holly was quiet, her face puckered into a frown as she considered her mother's advice. "I guess so," she agreed finally. "Next time I'll just tell him I think he's yucky."

Lauren chuckled at her five-year-old's logic. Still, she worried that if she didn't take a firm hand soon, Holly would grow up with Doug's lack of tact. He'd always prided himself so on being honest, sometimes brutally so. Lauren winced at the memory of the times he'd hurt her deeply with some thoughtless remark made under this personal banner of honesty at all costs.

Her marriage had not been a bad one despite that. Doug had been a friend and a good provider, even though he'd never been the sort of gentle, sensitive mate she'd dreamed of. Nor had he ever stirred her to great heights of passion, at least not the sort of uncontrolled desire about which she'd read. But they had had fun, sharing their many common interests, if not always their feelings. Both of them had been a little lonely, a little lost at college, and they had gravitated together in search of a companionship and warmth that had been missing from their childhoods.

That was what Lauren missed now more than anything—the companionship. Thank goodness for Holly, who chattered gaily about her childish concerns and filled the day's long hours with her need for attention. Without her, Lauren thought she might go slightly mad at being robbed of the one person who had ever given her a sense of belonging.

16

Certainly her parents had never done that. Her father had cared only about his work, or at least it had seemed so to her. And her mother wanted only to please her father. They had so completely ignored her, beyond providing the necessities, that when they were killed in a plane crash in the mountains of North Carolina during her freshman year at college, Lauren had barely missed them. She was determined that Holly would never feel as lost and alone as she had.

Later that night, after tucking Holly into bed and reading her a story, Lauren curled up in her own bed, prepared for another sleepless night, like so many of the others since Doug's death. But instead of tossing and turning, tormented by her loss and doubts about the future, she fell asleep almost immediately. Her dreams were filled this time, not with images of Doug, but of the tall, powerful stranger, whose anger at Reed Donovan had so shaken her earlier in the day.

CHAPTER TWO

When Lauren awoke in the morning, she felt more refreshed than she had in weeks, even though it was barely past daybreak. She walked to the tall, narrow windows of the attic room she and Doug had converted into a master bedroom suite and looked out at the tiny sliver of Charleston harbor visible in the distance. The water seemed especially blue on this crisp October morning, and the early sunlight bounced off the procession of stately mansions along the Battery

It was a sight that had never failed to charm her, dreamer that she was. It recalled the early days of this South Carolina port city, when women must have gazed for hours from the windows of those impressive houses, waiting to catch a glimpse of their men's ships sailing home. Today, as she stared out, a feeling of melancholy stole over her. Determined not to fall back into an all-too-familiar depression,

19

she forced herself to shower, slip on a pair of jeans and a bulky fisherman's knit sweater, and go down to begin breakfast and make plans for her last few days of freedom before she got caught up in the hectic schedule of work, classes, and caring for Holly.

The thought of once again filling up the hours of emptiness, of meeting people, of working toward her long-postponed dream of becoming an architect filled her with a sense of excitement and anticipation. As she sipped a cup of coffee, she spread out an assortment of folders on available classes, hoping to find one that would fit in with her work schedule. There was a three-hour seminar on Thursday evenings that seemed ideal. It was on a topic she cared about, urban planning, and she could trade baby-sitting with her neighbor in order to have the night free.

"Why are you smiling, Mommy," a little voice chirped at her side, interrupting her reverie.

"I'm just thinking how much fun it will be to go back to school," she said, pulling Holly into her lap for a hug. "And how's my favorite girl this morning?"

"Okay. Can I have some raisin cereal for breakfast?"

"You'd eat raisins in your scrambled eggs if I let you, wouldn't you, you little nut?"

"Not in my eggs, Mommy. That would be yucky."

"It's a relief to hear you say that. Now hop into that other chair so I can get up and get your cereal and some juice. You want apple juice or orange juice?"

"Apple," Holly replied, sitting down on the floor to tie her shoelaces yet again. Lauren smiled as she watched the look of intense concentration on Holly's face, which was framed by a halo of golden curls that gave her the look of a little cherub.

She really has her father's hair, Lauren thought thankfully, reaching up to touch her own straight, brown shoulder-length hair, which she'd gathered up in two jaunty ponytails. "Oh, well," she said with a sigh, "at least mine is thick and not baby fine."

"What's thick, Mommy?"

"What, honey? Oh, nothing. I was just thinking out loud, I guess. What would you like to do today? It's so beautiful out, I was thinking we might take a walk down to the park this morning. Would you like that?"

"Super! Can we stop for ice cream?"

"Holly, if you don't start thinking about something besides food, you're going to puff right up into a little pink pig. Anyway, it's too cold for ice cream."

As soon as Lauren had cleared away the breakfast dishes and given the house a quick dusting while Holly watched cartoons on TV, the pair started out toward the harbor. Absorbed in her own thoughts as she walked along holding Holly's hand, Lauren was startled by a frantic scream.

"Watch out!"

The next thing she knew a bicycle appeared practically at her side, swerving in order to miss her and Holly. As it turned sharply, it grazed the side of a parked car and flipped over, tossing its rider into the street.

"Are you hurt," Lauren asked breathlessly, rushing to where the man lay sprawled facedown in the street. Holly, her eyes wide with fright, stayed behind on the curb.

"Why, you little fool, we all could have been killed. Don't you know enough to watch where you're going!" The man exploded, his voice and its imperious tone jarring Lauren with its odd ring of familiarity. "I certainly hope they never let you behind the wheel of a car."

Reacting instinctively to the insult, she snapped back. "Who do you think you are? You're just as much at fault as I am. Why weren't you looking? Or is that too much to expect from a grown man of your obviously superior intelligence?"

"I was looking. If I hadn't been, you and the little one there would have been twisted up in the wheels of the bicycle or worse. My only mistake was in assuming that by your age you'd have learned to pay attention to traffic lights. I doubt you even knew one was up there."

Lauren's glance up proved the truth of his biting observation. But before he could make anything more of that, Holly moved protectively to Lauren's side.

"Why is the man yelling at you?" she asked. "He had a red light."

"What!" The shocked exclamation was made in unison by the two adults.

"Yes," Holly repeated with certainty, retreating to stand behind Lauren in the face of the man's doubting, scornful look.

"I always wait for the light before I cross the street. Mommy taught me to," she added for good measure, bringing a reluctant smile to the man's angular features.

"So," he said slowly, "I'm the one at fault after all." It sounded as though it wasn't the sort of admission he was used to making. Brushing himself off, he got to his feet and it was then, as he uncoiled that powerful body to tower over her, that Lauren realized why she had found the voice so familiar. It was Leland Cross.

Lauren allowed her eyes to travel up the trim, muscular body to meet his gaze. To her relief she found that the earlier disdain and anger had been replaced by a hint of amusement. Unable to look away, she felt as though she could drown in those penetrating gray eyes. Again, as she had the previous afternoon when she had first glimpsed Leland Cross in Reed Donovan's office, she shivered involuntarily.

Noticing her trembling, he attributed it to a delayed reaction to their accident and was instantly contrite. "Look, I really am sorry about all of this. You youngsters must be scared to death. I had visions of us all tangled up in a bloody heap under some car."

Lauren paled at the image he'd conjured up.

"Oh, no, now I'm only making it worse. Why don't we go over to that coffee shop and get something warm into you? It might make you feel better." Although the offer sounded sincere enough, Lauren felt as though she were being patronized and she resented it. She hesitated, taking Holly's hand and drawing her close.

"Please," he said beguilingly, giving her his most dazzling smile. "It would make me feel better."

Before Lauren could make up her mind, Holly piped up. "Will you buy me an ice cream cone?"

"Holly," Lauren said sharply as Leland Cross chuckled and knelt down in front of the little girl, who was eying him with the same mixture of interest and apprehension he inspired in her mother. In fact, Lauren had a hunch she should be running as far away from this compelling stranger as she could get.

But as her thoughts whirled, he was saying, "If you want an ice cream cone, then you shall have one. Just this once," he added, looking at Lauren's set face. "You deserve it for setting the record straight about our accident."

Lauren knew she could not decline now without seeming churlish. "All right," she agreed, noticing that Holly was already easing away from her to be closer to her newfound friend, whom she was entertaining with stories of kindergarten.

Fortunately, as they crossed the street to enter the restaurant on the corner, Holly had a limitless supply of tales and enthusiasm, for Lauren found herself tongue-tied, her senses reeling from the impact of Leland Cross and his raw animal magnetism. No man had ever had quite this effect on her, this instantaneous attraction that made her knees weak and her breath catch in her throat. Knowing that he was absorbed with Holly, she studied him closely, trying to analyze this seductive power he had over her.

Surely a part of it was the side of his personality she was seeing now, this gentle, attentive man who was so at odds with the domineering, quick-tempered Leland Cross she'd seen the day before. His gray eyes, which had seemed to go almost black with anger, twinkled dangerously now as he tried to hold back his laughter while he listened to Holly give her order for chocolate ice cream to the waitress who had appeared immediately after they sat down. He seemed genuinely delighted with his pint-sized companion and her observations.

But despite the more relaxed manner and his casual attire, he still exuded the same feeling of authority and control he had in his perfectly tailored three-piece suit. As Lauren's eyes came to rest on the tan chest exposed in the V of his blue velour shirt, her breathing became ragged. Just at that moment she caught Leland studying her quizzically as though trying to reconcile her instinctive sensual reaction to him with his impression of her as a scatterbrained teen-ager. She blushed furiously under the intensity of his gaze and looked away. Tremulously she began gathering up her purse and Holly's jacket.

"Come on, Holly," she insisted, her voice quivering in an infuriating manner that revealed far too much about her nervousness. "We've taken up enough of the gentleman's time."

"I've enjoyed it," he assured her. "Though I've a feeling I was so absorbed by this cute little kitten here, I completely missed out on the tigress beside her. Pull in your claws, my dear. No one's going to harm you."

The bantering tone and the sudden suggestiveness in his voice made Lauren even more uncomfortable. She had no idea how to cope with this sort of sexual undertone. But overriding her confusion in the face of his experience was her anger that he was so obviously amused at her expense.

"I'm so glad we've been able to provide an amusing diversion for you," she said haughtily. "It's unfortunate that your extensive educational background didn't include some lessons in manners."

"Was I being rude?" he asked innocently.

"You know very well you were," she said stiffly. "Holly, are you ready?"

"I guess so," she said, pouting at having her morning adventure cut short. Turning to Leland Cross, she said, "You will come and see us, won't you? You promised."

"Yes, I did promise. And I always keep my promises," he assured her, giving Lauren a look that carried a subtle warning. Her nerves tingled with an odd sense of anticipation. There was no doubt that her next encounter with Leland Cross, if there was one, would not be as harmless as this one.

Rattled by the certainty that this man was going to become inextricably involved in her future, Lauren dropped her purse, spilling the contents onto the floor. Her hands shaking, she jammed the things back into the purse, furious that she had so little control over her emotions. As she started for the door, Leland called out to her, forcing her to turn back. He was holding out her wallet, his laughter barely contained. She took it and ran, not hearing the booming laugh that followed her.

CHAPTER THREE

Late the following Friday afternoon, as Lauren was winding up her first week on the job, she returned from delivering some reports to the mayor to hear Leland Cross's voice echoing from her boss's office. By now she could recognize that deep, rich tone with its slight trace of a rough New York accent anywhere. She gazed apprehensively at the closed door as she returned to her desk to finish typing some letters Reed Donovan wanted to get out before the weekend. In her nervousness she managed to overturn a cup of coffee. Swearing softly under her breath, she tried to mop up the spill before it ruined the letters she'd already completed.

Mrs. Cates watched her curiously for a moment before asking, "What's the matter Lauren?"

"Nothing." She lied at first. But then seeing Mrs. Cates's disbelieving look, she said, "That's Leland Cross in there, isn't it?"

"Yes, but don't look so worried about it. At least he's not on a rampage for a change. Today will be a good day to meet him."

"I suppose so," she said uncertainly, turning back to the letters.

It was with a feeling of dread that she heard the office door open a few minutes later. When Reed spoke to her, she had a momentary flash of panic.

"Lauren, you're back just in time. There's someone here I'd like you to meet. Lee, this is Lauren Mitchell, who'll be taking over for Elsie."

Lauren turned around slowly, savoring the moment when the shock of recognition registered in those gray eyes. As she stared up at Leland Cross, he enveloped her small hand in his much larger one, holding it far longer than necessary. She wanted desperately to jerk it away, but she knew that to do so would be an admission that she was affected by his touch.

"Mr. Cross," she acknowledged softly.

"Ms. Mitchell," he said with a gallant bow, all the while massaging her palm sensuously with his thumb. "It's a pleasure to meet you."

His look became mocking as he added, "I trust Reed checked out your typing skills before he hired you. He has a way of letting a pretty face enchant him."

"I assure you . . ." Lauren began indignantly, but she was interrupted by Elsie Cates, who said soothingly, "Lauren is as thoroughly professional as she is beautiful, Mr. Cross."

"Then we should get along just fine, shouldn't we, Ms. Mitchell?"

28

There was a long moment of tension-packed silence as Lauren steeled herself to endure the challenge she saw in his eyes. Her own look was defiant; her green eyes flashed a dangerous warning of their own. He acknowledged her message with a barely perceptible nod and dropped her hand.

Elsie Cates and Reed Donovan watched the sparks flying between the two with some dismay. Not only did they not understand it, they were concerned about the effect of a personality clash between a city employee, particularly one right here in the planning office, and the city's most volatile and important developer. Elsie was the first to suspect that it might be something more than a clash of two strong wills. A romantic at heart, she smiled quietly, but wisely kept her observations to herself.

The long silence ended at last when Leland suggested, "Tell you what. Why don't I take Ms. Mitchell out for a cup of coffee and explain what it takes to get along with me? That may save a lot of wear and tear on her nerves in the long run."

The thought of being in close proximity to this virile, aggressive man brought a feeling of near panic to Lauren. She tried to refuse his offer, knowing he was merely taunting her by making it, but her boss wouldn't hear of it.

"Nonsense," Reed said, dismissing her excuses. "We can't afford to have the city's biggest developer unhappy, Lauren. You two run along. And, Lauren, you might as well go on home after that," he added generously.

"But I really do have to get those letters out,"

29

Lauren said again. This time it was Mrs. Cates who foiled her.

"I'll take care of the letters, honey. You've had a busy week, trying to learn everything around here and it's already late. You just go on with Mr. Cross and enjoy yourself. And have a nice weekend," she added, giving Lauren an encouraging push toward the door.

"All right. Thank you both," she said finally, trying to sound gracious, even though she felt they were throwing her to the wolves. Or to one wolf in particular anyway.

At least I look better today than I did on Saturday, she thought, then became angry at herself that she felt it mattered at all how she looked. *I'm not out to impress him,* she admonished herself, unwilling to admit even the possibility that she was.

Still, she was glad she was wearing her emerald silk blouse, which fell softly over her full breasts. Combined with a trim beige suit, accented with gold jewelry, it made her look like the polished young career woman she was instead of a sloppy teen-ager. She hadn't been able to afford many new clothes when she'd started job-hunting, so she'd chosen carefully. Her three new suits, all in muted tones, could be dressed up with the right accessories and the looks varied entirely, depending on the color of the blouses or scarves she wore with them. The emerald blouse, which emphasized the color of her eyes, was her favorite.

Funny how something as simple as the right blouse can give your confidence a boost, she thought, fully aware that for the next hour or so she was going to need every ounce of confidence she could muster up.

Already she could feel the tension beginning to build. The walk to the nearby restaurant seemed interminable. Leland said nothing, his expression stormy. He walked purposefully, like a man facing a distasteful task that he wanted to end in a hurry. He didn't even seem to notice that Lauren, nearly a foot shorter than he was, could barely keep pace with his long strides. And she was determined not to give him the satisfaction of pleading that he slow down.

By the time they reached the restaurant and were seated in a booth in a darkened corner, Lauren's nerves were on edge and she was growing more and more furious at his lack of sensitivity. As the silence between them became more and more prolonged, Leland made a calculatedly bold assessment of her, increasing her discomfort.

When he spoke at last, his tone was sarcastic. "So, it's Ms. Mitchell, is it?"

This open hostility was the last straw.

"What is the matter with you, Mr. Cross," she asked heatedly. "You act as though I've done something wrong and, frankly, I'm getting a little tired of your attitude."

"Are you really?" he asked coldly.

"I don't suppose you'd care to enlighten me about what I've done to you that is so terrible. We've barely met."

Before he could reply, the waitress appeared.

"I'd like a scotch on the rocks with a twist," he ordered, giving the attractive young girl his warmest smile. But the look he directed at Lauren was mocking, as he asked, "What about you, honey? A cup of hot chocolate?"

Lauren paled at his nasty tone. "I'll have a scotch as well," she said impulsively, determined not to be intimidated by his arrogance.

"Now then, Mr. Cross," she said once the waitress had brought their drinks. "You were about to explain what your insufferably rude behavior is all about."

"I don't need to explain anything to you."

"I think you do. I gather this has something to do with our encounter last weekend."

"The lady's a quick study," he said, lifting his drink in a mock salute.

"So? Finish the thought. Just how have I wronged you?"

The gray eyes stared at Lauren with an icy fierceness that startled and frightened her. His voice, when he spoke at last, was tightly controlled. "You made a fool of me, Ms. Mitchell. No one does that and gets away with it."

Lauren almost laughed aloud at the absurdity of the charge, but the look on his face stopped her. Fighting to maintain her composure, she managed to ask, "How on earth did I do that?"

"By coming on the other day like some sweet, innocent young child. You knew perfectly well I thought you were a terrified teen-ager."

"I hardly think I'm responsible, if you made an error in judgment. I certainly didn't try to deceive you."

"Didn't you? Why, if I had known you were fully grown, I would have . . ." His voice sputtered to an angry halt as their eyes locked. The moment went on and on, bringing with it an awareness that there was an undeniable attraction between them.

"You would have what?" Lauren pursued softly, still returning his gaze.

"I would have given you a good shaking," he said, his eyes contradicting his words as they came to rest on the sensuous curve of Lauren's full lips just as she moistened them nervously with the tip of her tongue.

"Are you sure that's what you would have done?" She teased Leland in a low, provocative voice, aware that it was the scotch that had made her irresponsibly daring. Instantly she regretted her remark, as a predatory gleam lit Leland's eyes and he continued his visual assault on her body.

"Can you think of a better way for me to get some satisfaction for that little act you put on?" he inquired suggestively, the intensity in his voice disturbing Lauren's pulse so profoundly that she looked away in confusion.

Fully aware of her reaction, he went on. "Perhaps I should come over this evening and we could try to work something out. After all, I did promise Holly I would visit. She is your little girl, not your sister, isn't she? I had that all wrong too."

Lauren nodded.

"About tonight," he prodded. "Can you get rid of your husband?"

"My husband is dead, Mr. Cross," she said, her temper flaring at his audacity. "But there is no way in hell I'd have you in my home."

"We'll see about that," he said, retreating gracefully. "I'm sorry about your husband, by the way. I didn't know."

"I think it's rather interesting, Mr. Cross, that before you found out about him, you had no qualms about committing adultery. My image really has been altered in your eyes, hasn't it? Just a few days ago you thought I was an untouchable young teenager. Now I'm fair game for anyone's attentions. Am I following your incredibly convoluted logic so far?" Her voice was filled with sarcasm. "Does this indicate your opinion of all women or is it just me?"

With that she dumped the remainder of her drink in his lap and fled. She was trembling as she made the ten-minute drive home, unable to keep the image of Leland Cross from her mind. The words that Reed Donovan had used to describe him, "a very determined young man," kept repeating themselves. At the pit of her stomach there was a feeling of revulsion and of fear. But, she realized, the fear was of her own emotions, which had gone crazy.

At home she made herself a cup of tea, hoping it would calm her down before she went next door to pick up Holly. As she sat sipping it, she kept seeing that rugged, tanned face and the determined set of his jaw. Leland Cross wanted her. There was no doubt about that. What she couldn't understand was why. And she wasn't being coy either. She knew she was attractive in an all-American, small town way. She had a nice figure, a good complexion, regular features, lovely eyes. It all added up to prom-queen beauty, not sophisticated glamor. Surely there were plenty of truly gorgeous women who would be Leland's for the asking.

So, why me, she asked herself again. *It must be that he thinks I'm a challenge. After all, he already feels I've made a fool of him once. Now he just wants to get even.*

Reaching that conclusion was small comfort for her. Knowledge of his motives would be little help in the face of his ruthless determination to get exactly what he wanted.

CHAPTER FOUR

Although Lauren found herself unconsciously holding her breath each time someone came into the office during the next few days, there were no more unsettling encounters with Leland Cross. In fact, there was nothing to mar her enjoyment of her new job and she was growing more certain daily that she would be able to handle things quite well beginning the following week, when Elsie Cates would be gone.

"What are you planning to do with all your unaccustomed free time, Elsie?" Lauren asked on Thursday as she was closing up the files for the day.

"Free time? Oh my, Lauren, I don't think I'll have all that much free time. I've got my garden club, my bridge club, the historical preservation group, and the women's aid society at church. Then there's Henry. He's determined that he's going to put me in fishing gear and take me out in that boat of his at the crack of dawn."

Lauren laughed at the look of distaste on her friend's face. "Come on, Elsie. That sounds like fun."

"Fun, my Aunt Tillie. Sitting out in a boat all morning long, putting shriveled-up old worms on the end of a hook. You call that fun?"

"Who are you trying to kid? You'll love every minute of it." Lauren chided her, thinking how much she'd come to love this spirited, kindly woman in just a few short days. Elsie Cates, with her matronly figure, her white hair, and easy smile, was exactly the sort of woman she wished she'd had as a mother. Lauren knew she would miss her terribly.

Now Elsie was saying, "Well, maybe I'll enjoy the part about spending more time with Henry, but I could live without the worms."

"Make Henry bait the hook for you then."

"Are you kidding? When it comes to fishing, Henry was an early women's libber. He believes anyone who can hold a fishing pole can manage to put the bait on it." She sighed in mock dismay. "Oh well, if togetherness in a rowboat will make Henry happy after all these years, I suppose I can manage somehow."

Lauren smiled wistfully. "You two really are something after all these years. How have you managed it, Elsie?"

"Managed what, honey?"

"Staying so happy. Most marriages these days either fall apart after a few years or drift along in some sort of emotional limbo until the end. But you and Henry really still seem to be in love after more than forty years together. It's incredible."

"Child, there's no secret in that. We do love each

other and we work at our marriage. Oh, I'm not saying that the sparks haven't flown through the years. A few of them have probably come pretty close to burning the whole thing down, but occasionally we've used them to light a fire, if you know what I mean," she said, a twinkle in her eye.

Noting Lauren's sad expression, she asked perceptively, "Weren't you and Doug happy?"

"Sometimes, yes," she said thoughtfully. "But I don't think we were ever as happy, even at first, as you and Henry are now. It seems like we missed out on so much."

"Well, your day will come. I'm sure there's someone out there who's just right for you and who'll make a fine father for Holly. Why, maybe you'll even meet him in this class you're starting tonight. It is tonight, isn't it?"

Lauren's face brightened with anticipation. "Yes, and I can hardly wait."

"Which class did you decide to take?"

"It's a seminar in urban planning. I thought it might help me out in here and it's something I might want to specialize in eventually."

"Urban planning? Isn't that the class—" Elsie began, an odd look on her face.

"Isn't that the class what, Elsie? What are you talking about?"

"Nothing, Lauren. I'm sure I must be mistaken."

That night, waiting in the classroom where the course was to be taught, Lauren found her own feelings of excitement reflected in the faces of the other students. There were only about twenty of them, most much younger than she. All but two of them we're men. The women, looking slightly uncomfortable and out of place, had gone to the back of the room as though hoping they wouldn't be noticed.

"Hi. Is this seat taken?" A tall, lanky young man was standing next to Lauren, looking down hopefully. She couldn't resist his eager expression.

"No. Have a seat. My name's Lauren Mitchell."

"Rod Stevens, Lauren," he said, grinning and reaching to shake her hand. His books spilled from his arms in the process, causing him to flush a bright red in embarrassment.

"You'll discover I have a tendency toward clumsiness, especially around pretty women. Sure it's still okay, if I sit down?"

"Absolutely. I drop things all the time too. We can pick up after each other," she said, smiling easily.

"I haven't seen you around before. Did you just start taking classes here?"

"Yes. This is my first one. I've been away from college for a while and I'm trying to get started again."

"You picked a tough class to start with," he said, his slow drawl identifying him as a local boy.

"Oh? Why?"

"Because of the instructor. He's a real terror according to all survivors of his classes. He's a perfectionist. He only teaches this class once a year and, as you can see, the classroom is not exactly overcrowded. It takes a brave soul to try it."

"Why are you here, if it's all that terrible?"

"Because he's the best and I want to learn. I guess I can put up with a few tantrums in exchange for some valuable training. Uh-oh. There he is now," he said, his voice dropping to a whisper.

Lauren looked toward the door and saw Leland standing there talking to another teacher. Somehow she knew she should have expected it, but she hadn't.

"Oh, my God," she said softly, trying to sink down and make herself inconspicuous. She knew, though, that it was a futile effort in a room this size. Sooner or later he would spot her, and there was no telling what would happen when he did.

"Hey, are you okay," Rod asked gently. "You've gone pale all of a sudden. You aren't going to faint on me, are you?"

Lauren tried to smile reassuringly. "No. Don't worry. I'll be just fine. I just felt a little dizzy for a minute."

As Leland stood before the class, dressed casually in tan slacks, a striped shirt, and darker brown V-necked sweater, he appeared as much in command of himself and the situation as ever. Lauren found herself fascinated with the pulse she could see beating in his neck. She felt as though her own heart were about to burst in an effort to match its pace. Her thoughts raced as well, as she tried to anticipate his reaction when he spotted her.

But to her surprise, although his eyes surveyed the room, he did not look directly at her once. Feeling safer, she was able to relax and listen to his lecture, her excitement growing with each passing moment. Rod had been right. Lee knew his subject and he was an impassioned speaker. He conveyed in dramatic terms the plight facing cities, the problems of un-

41

checked urban sprawl and poor planning, and the responsibilities of civic leaders, residents, and developers to work together to create an atmosphere for change and growth.

Scribbling notes as quickly as she could, Lauren made some accompanying sketches to match the roughly drawn illustrations Leland had done on the blackboard. Her hand ached from trying to keep up. Glancing at Rod, she saw that he shared her excitement and her weariness.

Then, suddenly, it was over.

"Next week I would like each of you to come prepared to discuss how you would handle the following problems, both in terms of building design and of dealing with city planning regulations," he said, his eyes raking over the class to stop at the two young women in the back. He gave them his most charming grin and Lauren seethed with an unaccountable feeling of jealousy.

He ticked off the details for the assignment rapidly, then dismissed the class.

"Whew," Rod whispered to Lauren. "See what I mean? He's everything I'd heard and then some, a real dynamo. Don't you think so?"

"He's good all right." Lauren agreed absentmindedly, wondering how she was going to escape from the room without meeting him. She didn't have to wonder long.

"Ms. Mitchell, I'd like to see you for a moment, please."

The politeness of his statement did not mask the command in his voice. He expected to be obeyed. Bristling at the order, but unable to think of a way to avoid the confrontation, Lauren gathered up her things, trying to ignore Rod's questioning look.

"Do you want me to wait for you?" he asked.

"No. I don't think so. But thanks," she said, giving him a friendly pat on the arm. "I'll see you next week."

"Okay. If you're sure," he said, waving as he left.

Lauren took her time going up to Leland's desk, but even so, he remained occupied with paperwork As he continued to ignore her, she grew impatient, but it was not until the last of the students left that he looked up.

"Following me around, Ms. Mitchell?" he asked, his tone only mildly curious. "I was under the impression you were terrified to be near me."

"Terrified, Mr. Cross? Whatever gave you that impression? You don't scare me, though your manners and your ego appall me at times."

"Is that so?" he asked doubtfully, then shrugged and changed the subject. "Just why are you in this class?"

"For the same reason as the rest of the students, I imagine. To learn."

"Oh?" His look was skeptical as he took her notebook from her and flipped the pages. Stopping at her sketches, he studied them closely and nodded. "Not bad. You have a nice touch."

"Thanks."

"As for what I can teach you, I agree there are certain lessons you need to learn, but I'm not sure this is the appropriate atmosphere. Why don't we adjourn to someplace more comfortable and I can share a few of my ideas with you?"

"I'm not interested in your ideas on anything besides urban planning, Mr. Cross," she insisted savagely.

"Oh, I'm sure I can manage to arouse your interest, my dear," he said, taking her arm in a painful grip and escorting her from the room. When they reached the parking lot, he began to steer her toward his low-slung sports car.

"Mr. Cross, I do not need a ride. I have my car here," she said, trying to release herself from his grasp.

"You can pick it up tomorrow," he said, ignoring her struggling.

"Mr. Cross," she said with exasperation, "I do not have time to chase all over town in the morning to get my car. I have a job, in case you've forgotten."

"Ah, yes. What would the planning department do without its able, new secretary? Fine. You may drive your own car. But, Lauren," he said, his tone deadly serious, "I will be right behind you. You and I are going to have a talk tonight. Understand?"

Knowing it was hopeless to argue, she replied listlessly, "Yes. I understand. But I will have to stop next door first and pick up Holly and get her to bed. It should only take a few minutes."

"Okay," he agreed, opening the door of her gas-saving compact for her. "I'll follow you and wait until you pick up Holly."

Even without his final reminder, Lauren would have been aware of the sports car, its power held in check, as it followed her to the neighborhood of old brick mansions and carriage houses where she lived.

At Sue's she was so nervous that she dropped her

44

keys, then her purse, causing her friend to look at her oddly.

"Lauren, are you okay?" she asked with concern. "Holly can spend the night here, if you're not feeling well."

"Sue, I'm fine," she snapped, then apologized. "Look, it's been a long day and I'm worn out. That's all. I'll be just fine."

"How did the class go?"

"Sue, not tonight, please. We'll talk about it tomorrow. Thanks for looking after Holly for me," she said, cutting off further conversation. Lauren knew that her abrupt behavior was worrying Sue, but she couldn't handle any more questions. She did pause to give Sue a reassuring hug. "Don't worry about me. I'll be fine in the morning."

As she walked across the path to her converted carriage house, Leland stepped from his car and came to meet her. He took the sleeping Holly from her arms, then waited while Lauren opened the door and turned on the lights.

"Where does she go?" he asked, his expression gentle as he gazed down at the child who'd nestled down in his arms, a look of perfect contentment on her face.

"This way," Lauren said, leading him to the tiny room that had been decorated in brightly patterned wallpaper.

Stepping over the toys strewn all over the floor, he put Holly down on her bed and removed her coat carefully, trying not to wake her in the process. Snuggling down under the covers with her favorite doll, Holly opened her eyes briefly, took in the darkly handsome man looking tenderly down at her, and smiled an angelic smile.

"Hi," she whispered sleepily. "I knew you'd come." Then she sighed with pleasure and went back to sleep. Leland stood watching her, plainly reluctant to leave the room. Finally he too sighed, a little wistfully it seemed to Lauren, and walked back to the living room.

Lauren's trepidation about being alone with Leland came flooding back now. She began to chatter nervously, saying whatever came into her head, as she paced the living room, avoiding his watchful eyes. She heard his low chuckle of amusement when she finally wound down, and a feeling of panic engulfed her. Frantically she darted toward the kitchen, calling out, "Would you like some coffee? Or a drink? I'm not sure what I have here."

"You have all I want right here," a voice said right behind her, startling her. She turned sharply and found herself in Leland's arms, which tightened around her immediately. She tried to fight the sensations aroused by his embrace, the desire to bury her face in his shoulder and cling to him, breathing deeply of his warm, musky male scent.

"Mr. Cross . . ." she began determinedly, twisting in his arms to widen the space between their bodies.

"Lee," he insisted, his eyes twinkling.

"All right. Lee, I really think you have the wrong idea about me."

"Oh? Exactly what idea do you think I have?" he asked, nuzzling her neck in a way that sent a tingling down her spine.

"You're . . . you're," she said, gasping as his

tongue lightly touched her ear. "You're just trying to get even with me. You think I deliberately did something to you."

"Well, I don't know if it was deliberate, but you *have* done something to me. You've made it impossible for me to get you out of my mind. When that happens, there's only one thing left to do," he said ominously, his face descending toward hers.

"No. Please," she pleaded, struggling to get free.

"Which is it? No or please," he teased, his lips coming down to meet hers, touching with a feathery softness that made her lean weakly against him. When he increased the pressure, forcing her lips apart, his tongue invading the sweetness of her mouth, an unfamiliar warmth spread through her body and she moved even closer to him. Sensing her near-capitulation, he moved his hands expertly over her, tracing a pathway of fire along her bare skin. When her arms, no longer able or willing to fight him, crept up and around his neck, he swept her up in his muscular arms and carried her back to the living room.

His lips never left hers as he stretched her out gently on the sofa, then lowered himself on top of her, positioning one long, hard leg between her thighs. A warning light flashed briefly in Lauren's mind, signaling for her to stop now, while she had the chance, before the situation got completely out of control. But she could not force the words from her mouth. Her traitorous body was in tune with Leland's, arching to meet his.

With the effortlessness of experience, he stripped away her blouse and unhooked her bra, freeing her

47

breasts for the onslaught of his gentle kisses. The nipples hardened immediately and Lauren gasped with unexpected pleasure as she was stirred by the unfamiliar sensations caused by his massaging and stroking.

Lauren allowed the feelings to wash over her in tingling waves. Her breath came in ragged gulps as his hands explored lower and lower. Her body was on fire and it was like no experience she had ever had before. Certainly Doug had never had this power to possess her, to carry her along to the heights of passion. Doug, with his gentle, undemanding touch, his own low expectations, had never stirred her like this.

Suddenly Lauren froze as the memories of Doug came roaring back, blocking the impact of Leland's expert lovemaking. What was she doing here, a voice seemed to be screaming inside her head. How could she allow a virtual stranger to make this assault on her body? What kind of a woman was she?

Then she was screaming, pleading with Leland to stop. When he persisted, she twisted beneath him, pounding on his shoulders with frantic fists. "No, Lee. Please, no."

Tears were streaming down Lauren's face and Leland must have tasted their saltiness as he trailed kisses along her cheeks and throat. Finally he stopped, their passion over as quickly as it had flared, and he stood looking down at her.

There was a look of rage mingled with confusion on his face.

"Why, Lauren?" he asked softly.

She shook her head, sobbing quietly.

"Damn you for this," he swore quietly as he snatched up his jacket and left.

Lauren, the memory of the expression of scorn on his face searing through her heart, huddled, shivering, in a corner of the sofa and cried as though her heart would break.

CHAPTER FIVE

"Ms. Mitchell, it's Leland Cross." The voice on the phone was cool and detached. "Let me talk to Reed, please."

Lauren's hands were shaking and she was gripping the phone so tightly her knuckles were white. Taking a deep breath, she tried to match his professional tone.

"He's not here just now, Mr. Cross. Would you care to leave a message?"

"Yes. Tell him I need to speak with him immediately. When do you think he'll be back?"

"He's with the mayor right now, but he should be back in his office within the hour."

"I should still be in my office then, but if I've left, ask him to have my secretary locate me immediately. As I said, this is urgent."

"Fine. I'll see that he gets the message. Will that be all?" she asked politely.

"No. There's something else."

"What?" she asked curtly, no longer trying to hide her desire to end the conversation.

"Will you be in class tonight?"

The sudden shift to a more personal subject only increased Lauren's nervousness. She was not ready to face Leland Cross. This phone call, their first contact since he had stormed from her home the previous week, certainly proved that.

"I'm not sure," she told him at last. "I haven't decided yet."

There was a touch of annoyance in Leland's response. "Lauren, you can't let what happened the other night keep you away from the class. It's simply not necessary."

"I think perhaps it is," she answered truthfully.

"Why?"

When she didn't respond, he went on. "Lauren, we are both adults. We made a mistake. Let's just admit that and forget it."

"I'm not sure I can do that, Mr. Cross. However, you are right about one thing. What happened was a tremendous mistake. I intend to make certain it isn't repeated."

"It won't be. Now I expect you to be in class tonight. We'll talk about it some more afterward. Okay?"

"I'll think about it," she hedged.

"Just be there, Lauren. If you're not, I'll simply have to come looking for you."

For the remainder of the day Lauren debated what she should do. Despite what had happened between them, she felt no real anger toward Leland Cross.

She was as much to blame as he was. She had invited his caresses or at least she had done nothing to turn them away. Then when she had suddenly changed her mind, it should not have surprised her that he was furious.

The real issue, however, was whether she was willing to risk another assault on her already shaky emotions. It was obvious Leland had the ability to arouse her. A slow, sensual smile or a tender touch and her body would betray her again. She was certain of it. How long could she possibly hold out before making a second dreadful mistake and tumbling into bed with him? A casual affair was no solution to the unexplained yearnings she had been feeling for so long now. She wanted more than mere physical gratification. She wanted love as well. That, she knew, was the last thing Leland was offering her.

Lauren wished she had someone to talk to about her confusion. As close as she felt to Sue, she had never shared intimate confidences with her. Perhaps feeling rejected by her parents as a child had left her incapable of revealing her innermost thoughts to anyone. She didn't want anyone to know just how truly vulnerable she was.

This time, however, Lauren was almost tempted to break her code of silence. When she had dropped Holly off next door, Sue had seen how troubled she was and had tried to coax her into talking.

"Honey, I've never seen you like this. Even when Doug died, you didn't seem this withdrawn. I thought you'd be thrilled about getting back to school, but instead you came in here last Thursday after class shaking like a leaf. Tonight you look as though I'm sending you off to an execution. What gives?"

"Oh, Sue, I can't explain it. It's not really the class. That's wonderful. I really do think I'll learn a lot. But there are some other things I just have to work out for myself. I appreciate your caring, though," she said, giving Sue a quick hug. "I won't be too late tonight."

"Don't worry about that. If somebody wonderful asks you out after class, just give me a call. Holly can spend the night here."

"Thanks. You're a love."

Several times on the way to class Lauren nearly turned back, but some force seemed to be pushing her on. She tried to convince herself it was because she could never explain to Sue why she had returned home, but she knew it was more than that. A part of her wanted to be in that class tonight. Any chance of escape was ended in the parking lot, when Rod Stevens spotted her and walked over to meet her.

"Hi," he called out. Rod took Lauren's arm politely as he joined her and they walked to the classroom together. "I'm glad to see Mr. Cross didn't scare you away."

The implication of the comment startled Lauren, until she realized Rod couldn't possibly know about what had happened after class. Her guilt was making her a little crazy.

"What did he want to see you about anyway?" Rod asked curiously.

"Oh, nothing terribly important. He just wanted to know if I was the same Lauren Mitchell, who'd just gone to work in the city planning department," she improvised quickly. She was not willing to admit, even to Rod, that the meeting had been more personal.

"And are you? The same Lauren Mitchell, I mean?"

"Yes. I've just been there a couple of weeks now."

"What do you do?" Rod asked with evident interest. "That must be a great place to work for someone interested in architecture and urban planning."

"It is. But I'm only a lowly secretary, nothing exciting."

"Well, obviously you don't intend to remain a secretary if you're taking this class."

"No. I do want that architecture degree I started on years ago. It may take forever, though, since I can only take classes at night and on weekends."

"I know what you mean," he sympathized. "I'm doing it that way too. But why don't you go back full-time, or is that one of those dumb questions with an obvious answer?"

"It's not a dumb question, but the answer is the usual one. Money. I've got a daughter to support," she said without the slightest trace of bitterness or self-pity.

"That must be rough. Are you divorced?"

At the look of sadness that crossed her face, he added quickly, "Hey, if I'm being too nosy, just tell me to mind my own business. Occasionally I have to be put in my place."

"I'll remember that," Lauren said, laughing. "But the question's okay. I'm a widow. My husband died last spring."

"Oh," he said, silenced for a moment. "Listen,

Lauren, if you ever need a man around to help out, just let me know."

Lauren gave him a sharp look, expecting to find the leer that usually accompanied such offers. It wasn't there. Rod, however, apparently sensed her thoughts, for he continued. "I'll bet you've had a few offers like that before, haven't you? And some of them probably turned out to be more than you bargained for, right?"

Lauren nodded.

"Well, I meant just what I said. Nothing more. If you need someone, as a friend, I'll be available."

"Thanks," she said, touched by his sincerity and his sensitivity.

"Look, why don't you come with us for coffee after class? Three or four of us were planning to go to a little place right up the road to unwind a little."

"That sounds like fun. I would like to meet some of the others in the class. I'll only be able to stay for a little while, though," she warned. "I don't want to leave Holly at my neighbor's too late."

"No problem. You can cut out whenever you need to."

Lauren flashed him a grateful smile, which froze on her face as she looked up to see Leland motioning for her to come to his desk. Embarrassed at being singled out for the second week in a row, she fought to keep her anger under control as she approached him. It wouldn't do to flare up right in front of everyone.

"What do you want, Mr. Cross?" she hissed sharply under her breath. "I really don't think it's particularly considerate for you to use class time to perse-cute me."

"I hardly think that's what I'm doing, Lauren. I just want us to get along. If you'll join me for a drink after class, we can talk about it further."

"I'm sorry. I have other plans," she said stiffly.

"Change them," he ordered.

"No!"

"Lauren," he said, his voice taking on a dangerous edge, "change your plans. I want to get this matter settled tonight."

"And I told you that I will not change my plans to suit you," she said flatly, turning and marching back to her seat.

"What on earth was that about?" Rod whispered as Lauren sat down. "He looks as though he's ready to tear the place down."

Lauren shrugged indifferently and opened her notebook, hoping that Rod wouldn't notice that her eyes were smarting with tears. She hated these little scenes with Leland. They were chipping away at her emotions, leaving them raw and vulnerable.

For the next three hours she was almost able to push everything that had happened aside, as she struggled to keep up with Leland's lecture. He tore through it at a frenzied pace, not bothering to hide his rage. Whenever a student was slow to respond to his relentless questioning, he reacted with biting sarcasm. By the end of the evening everyone was ter-rified to speak up at all.

Finally, casting them all a look of total disgust, he walked to his desk, shoved his papers into his attaché case, and stormed out of the room, leaving the class sitting in shocked silence.

"Whew! I'd heard he had a bad temper, but I didn't expect anything like this," Rod said to Lauren. "What on earth was bothering him tonight, I wonder. Do you have any idea, Lauren? You talked to him before class. Was he in a foul mood then?"

"From what I've seen of Leland Cross, he spends most of his time in a foul mood," she said lightly. "Perhaps tonight he just felt he should share it with us."

The other woman, who'd been subjected to a particularly brutal attack during the lecture, came over to join them.

"At least we're prepared now," she offered. "Surely it won't ever be any worse than this."

"Let's hope not," Rod agreed as they left for the nearby diner.

Despite feeling emotionally battle-weary from Leland's classroom tirade, Lauren was determined to enjoy the rest of the evening. Over the next hour the events of the last six years seemed to slip away and she felt as though she were back in college. It was good to have young people to talk to again, especially people who shared her interests. For too long now she had been locked into a restricted environment in which the chief topics of discussion had been ways to fix hamburger, how to shave a few dollars from the electric bill, or which kindergarten offered the best education.

For a while she sat in silent enjoyment, letting the conversation flow over her. Suddenly the talk turned to Leland Cross and his planned office tower on the waterfront.

"You work in the city planning office, Lauren. What do you think its chances are for approval?" Rod asked.

"I don't really know too much about it," she replied truthfully. "It's been mentioned a couple of times, but I'm not even sure where it's supposed to go or what it will look like."

"It's the most exciting thing that's happened to this town in a hundred years," an aggressive young man named Dave Findlay offered enthusiastically. "It's going to be thirty stories high, all glass and steel, overlooking the harbor. We'll finally have a skyline and maybe this will be the beginning of some real urban growth in Charleston."

"Come on, Dave. You don't have to have skyscrapers and ruin your waterfront to have progress," Rod replied heatedly. "Charleston has struggled to maintain a certain way of life."

"Yeah. Backward," muttered Dave.

"It's not backward to want the city to have a certain character, a flavor that will remind everyone of the city's history. Charleston radiates the sort of old-fashioned southern hospitality that a lot of people long for. It has charm now. What will it have if Leland Cross has his way? It won't be a bit different from any other city in the country. As much as I admire Cross as a developer, I think he's way off target with this one. I just pray the city won't cave in to his pressure."

"You sound like one of those little old ladies from the preservation society," Dave charged.

"The group is not just a bunch of little old ladies. The members are people who care about Charleston," Rod retorted.

"They're living in the past, I tell you."

"Dave," Rod began patiently. "Don't you see that what has put Charleston on the map has nothing to do with tall buildings? Tourists come here because it is different. And the Spoleto festival every spring would never have happened if this were some backward cultural wasteland. Why, original works by some of the top playwrights and composers in the world have been introduced right here."

"I still say the time is right to start opening the city up to projects that will bring in millions of dollars in new businesses," Dave said, refusing to cave in to Rod's arguments.

"Why can't you do both?" Lauren asked. "Isn't it possible to design a structure that won't mar the city's character and will still attract major investors to the area?"

"Of course it is, Lauren," Rod said. "But there is another problem with the Cross building that has nothing to do with the way it looks."

"What's that?"

"Where he wants to put it. He has an option on some prime land right along the harbor, land that the city had wanted for a park. To complicate it even more, there are a couple of buildings there now that the preservationists want to have declared as national historic landmarks, which means they couldn't be torn down."

"That's what you meant when you were asking about the zoning approval? But why would the city

60

be likely to give him the approval, if it wants the land for itself?"

"Money, my innocent. The city was negotiating for the property when Leland Cross came along and offered the owner big bucks if he could get the zoning approved. Now the owner wants to forget all about the proposed deal with the city. He's even offered them free alternative land for a park if they'll go along on this."

"Couldn't it be done the other way around? Get Leland Cross to take the other land and leave the waterfront available as a park?"

Rod gave a harsh laugh. "Cross won't do it. He's adamant about having his tower on the waterfront."

Lauren remembered a snatch of the conversation she'd heard in Reed Donovan's office the day she had applied for her job. Leland had been complaining about the city officials suddenly going protective about their waterfront. *So,* she thought, *that's what it was all about.*

The conversation took another twist finally and Lauren glanced at her watch, surprised to see that it was after midnight. Thankful that she had called Sue earlier and let her neighbor talk her into letting Holly sleep over, she decided it was still time to call it a night. Otherwise she'd be worn out at the office in the morning.

On the drive home she thought over everything she'd heard tonight about Leland's plans. She was not surprised at his stubbornness. Certainly she had seen enough evidence that he could be ruthless when it suited his purposes. But it saddened her to think of what he had planned for the waterfront. Once that property was zoned for a high-rise office building, it wouldn't be long before more would follow. When that happened, there would be no turning back.

She thought of a visit she'd made to Chicago years before with her parents. Somehow the city had planned early and well to preserve the Lake Michigan shoreline. A wide multilane drive separated the beach from towering apartments and offices along one stretch, and Lincoln Park edged the water for miles more. It made the masses of steel, glass, and concrete that rose in unending columns downtown seem less forbidding. It offered a touch of suburban greenery in the midst of the usual urban color scheme of gray and black.

Lauren prayed the Charleston officials would have the presence of mind to plan as well.

CHAPTER SIX

Even though Lauren arrived at the office earlier than usual the following morning, she found Leland there ahead of her, his face set in an expressionless mask.

"Mr. Cross, what are you doing here at this hour?" she asked, irritated that her pulse seemed to be beating erratically at the sight of him. "Mr. Donovan won't be here for at least another half-hour."

"I know that. I'm here to see you."

"Me?" She sat down quickly, hoping he wouldn't notice that she was trembling.

"Yes, and don't act so surprised. I told you yesterday that you and I needed to have a talk. Since you chose not to have it last night, I thought we'd just get it out of the way this morning."

"I'm sorry. That's not possible. Someone may come in," she said lamely. "Besides, I don't see what you and I have to discuss. I came back to class, as you insisted. I won't drop out. What more do you want?"

"I'm glad you decided to stay in the course, but that's not really the issue, and you know it," he said, his tone reflecting his annoyance. He gave her a penetrating look, as though trying to decide why she was being deliberately difficult.

Suddenly, though, the look changed as Leland boldly assessed Lauren from head to foot, his eyes coming to rest on her quivering lips. A trace of a smile lifted the corners of his mouth and his gaze rose to meet hers. Despite the unsettling impact of that look, Lauren was unable to turn away and the familiar spark of electricity crackled between them.

Leland got up from his chair and came around to stand towering over Lauren, his eyes never leaving hers. It was with a feeling of inevitability that Lauren saw his face moving closer and closer until his soft lips brushed hers. When she would have swiveled her chair away from him, she found herself imprisoned by his arms, which lifted her to her feet. As his kiss deepened, he pulled her closer, until her body was molded to his. She could feel the pounding of his heart, which echoed her own.

Then, just as she reached up to put her hands in his thick, black hair, no longer able to ignore the attraction she felt for him, he set her gently away and walked back to the other side of the desk. Lauren tried to steady her uneven breathing and to put aside the feeling of loss which overcame her.

She gave him a puzzled glance.

"You may be right," he said at last, his voice husky. "This isn't the place for us to talk. I don't seem to be able to keep my hands off you, and since I'm unlikely to learn self-restraint while you're around, we'd better have our meeting in private. I will pick you up for dinner tonight at seven."

Without waiting for her reply, he left, leaving Lauren with a stunned expression on her face. Her initial anger at his arrogant assumption that she would have dinner with him gave way to her desire to see him. But, as she had the previous day, she warred with herself against capitulating. She knew the danger of seeing him in an intimate setting. Good grief, she couldn't even control herself in her office. How could she dare risk being alone with him at home?

At last she decided on a compromise, one she was sure would infuriate him. The thought gave her a certain amount of delight. She would insist that Holly accompany them. It wasn't much in the way of protection, but it was better than nothing.

Holly could barely contain herself when Lauren told her they would be having dinner with Leland. When the doorbell rang promptly at seven, she ran to answer it.

"Mommy, he's here. It's Lee," she announced excitedly, hurling herself into his waiting arms.

"Hi, pumpkin. How are you?" he asked, his face lit with a genuinely tender smile.

"I'm fine. You came to see me the other night, when I was asleep, didn't you?"

"I sure did. I'm surprised you remember."

"How come you didn't wait until I woke up in the morning?" she asked, her voice accusing as she stood in front of him, hands on her tiny hips. Lauren blushed at the question and Leland grinned with delight.

"Maybe next time I will," he said wickedly, laughing at the murderous expression that passed over Lauren's face. "How about it, Lauren?"

Before she could answer, Holly interrupted. "Guess what, Lee? Mommy said I could have dinner with you tonight. Where are we going?"

Leland cast Lauren a furious glance, but he recovered quickly.

"Well," he began slowly, "I'd had something a little fancy in mind, but I suppose we can adjust that."

For the first time Lauren noticed that he was wearing a dark, three-piece suit and a crisply starched white shirt. For an instant she felt guilty at spoiling his plans. Leland, however, didn't seem the least bit troubled by the turn of events.

"How about Italian food," he asked Holly. "Can I interest you in some spaghetti or a pizza, little one? Maybe we can try to fatten your mommy up a little."

"I lo-o-o-ve spaghetti," Holly said with feeling. "But I bet we can't find any that's as good as Mommy's. She makes super spaghetti."

"Well, next time we'll have her make dinner in that case. But tonight it's on me."

Lauren was disconcerted at the ease with which Leland had adapted to the change in plans. By the time she had picked up her purse and a jacket for Holly, he had removed his jacket, vest, and tie. His shirt collar was open and he had rolled up his sleeves. He looked devastatingly handsome.

At the restaurant, a neighborhood, family-style

place that was filled with teen-agers and young couples with small children, Leland seemed perfectly comfortable. In fact, for a few minutes Lauren even daydreamed of what it would be like if they were a real family, just like the others around them. Leland caught her wistful expression and smiled knowingly, causing Lauren to blush. She had the uncanny feeling that he did know exactly what she had been thinking.

Lauren was glad to see the relationship that was springing up between Leland and Holly. Holly had not talked much about her father, but Lauren knew she had felt the pain of his death. It was good that Leland had found a place in Holly's heart. For his part, he seemed to accept the role of surrogate father quite naturally, even to the point of disciplining her when she became overly boisterous and difficult as the evening wore on and she got tired.

Back at the house Holly insisted on having Leland put her to bed and read her a story. After she'd been tucked in for the night, had a drink of water and a kiss, she allowed Leland to leave and join Lauren in the living room, where she was curled up on the floor in front of the fire.

Leland fixed them both a brandy and stretched out next to Lauren, his back leaning up against the sofa. He sighed.

"This is nice. I can't think of the last time I felt so relaxed," he said.

"You really like being with Holly, don't you?"

"She's a wonderful little girl. I've always wanted a family, but things just haven't worked out," he replied a little wistfully. "I guess I've been married to my work for so long I'd forgotten it couldn't give me children. I guess it's too late now."

"Why on earth would you think that?" Lauren demanded. "You're not that old. What are you? Thirty-four? Thirty-five?"

"I'm thirty-five and I agree that's not old, but there are other things it's just too late to change."

"For instance?"

Leland gave her a long, hard look before turning back to gaze thoughtfully into the fire. At last he spoke and his voice was filled with the pain of long-forgotten memories.

"I learned one thing from my childhood, Lauren. A father owes his family more than money Mine certainly never gave us anything except an allowance, a very generous allowance. It was supposed to make up for all the time he was away at work. I would have given anything if he'd taken me fishing or to a ballgame."

Lauren nodded, her expression understanding. She wanted to reach out and touch him, to take away some of the hurt that little boy had felt. Instead, she said, "It sounds to me as though the lesson you learned from all that would make you a very good father. My family was the same way. I don't think my father ever took off a day just to be with us. Even at home he was always on the phone making deals. But I think that experience has made me a better mother, at least I hope it has."

"Yes, but you don't have a career that makes constant demands on your time," Leland argued, ignoring Lauren's warning that he was sounding chauvinistic. "You can leave the office at the end of the day and know that you don't have to worry about it again until the following morning. When you're the one in charge, that's impossible. There are too many people relying on you. If you've got any sense of responsibility at all, you can't just walk away at the end of an eight-hour day and pretend it doesn't exist."

"So you decided to sacrifice having any family life at all?"

"I'm not sure I ever made that decision consciously, but, yes, I guess that's exactly what I've done. I've tended to gravitate toward women who were high achievers in their own professions, knowing that they would never impose too many demands on my time."

"Have there been a lot of them?" Lauren asked before she could stop herself.

Leland gave her a sharp look as she held her breath waiting for his reply

"Jealous?" he asked with a devilish grin.

"No way," she said indignantly, hoping he wouldn't detect the lie in her denial. "I'm just curious. I would think that even high achievers, as you call them, might fall under your spell sooner or later and want more than you're prepared to give."

"I manage to avoid that possibility."

"How? By shifting your affections quickly and frequently?"

"Very perceptive. But that's enough about my love life. What about yours?" he asked, lifting her hand to his lips for a fleeting kiss. The touch lasted no longer than a fragile, melting snowflake, but it affected Lauren deeply with its tenderness. She tried to laugh to cover her nervousness, but the sound seemed strained and artificial.

"I'm afraid single mothers don't have much of a love life, especially if they're trying to work and go to school at the same time. Besides . . ." She couldn't complete the sentence.

"Besides, it's too soon after your husband's death. Is that it?"

She nodded. Leland's look was sympathetic. "I think I can understand that. That's what the other night was all about, wasn't it?"

"Yes. I just . . . I just couldn't go through with it. It seemed, I don't know, a little like a betrayal. There's a part of me that still feels married. Doug tried so hard. It wasn't his fault that I felt that something was missing in our lives."

"Are you planning to pay him back for whatever he did by devoting the rest of your life to his memory? Lauren, that would be such a waste, and if Doug was the sort of man you say he was, he wouldn't want that for you."

"I know you're right, but being with another man, with you so soon, it seemed as though I were being disloyal."

Lauren was surprised that she had revealed so much. She didn't realize that tears were rolling down her cheeks as she talked until Leland brushed them away. Then he took her in his arms and held her, making no demands, just offering her the comfort of his presence. Soothingly he stroked her hair, which sparkled with red highlights from the fire's glow. Lauren felt more protected than she ever had in her life.

But when he sensed that she was calm, Leland withdrew his arms and got to his feet. When he'd picked up his jacket, vest, and tie, he leaned down to give Lauren a quick kiss on the forehead.

"You're leaving? But why?"

"We'll talk about it another time, Lauren. Not tonight," he said, his tone harsh and final. She recognized the finality and accepted it, but she couldn't stop the feeling of abandonment that assailed her as he walked out the door.

Nothing that happened over the next couple of weeks clarified just why he had left so abruptly that night and, not knowing, Lauren was miserable. But she fought to hide her confusion, thankful that she had the routine of work and Holly to keep her mind occupied.

On the few occasions that Leland had called the office, he had been courteous but impersonal. In class he showed complete impartiality, calling on her no less or more than he did the others. There were no special looks, no requests for her to remain after class. In fact, she began to sense that his hurried departures at the conclusion of his lectures were only to prevent any possible confrontation with her.

Instead of lessening, Lauren's bewilderment only grew. She tried to convince herself that she was grateful he was no longer pursuing her, but, instead, she felt lonely and betrayed. More than that, she hated the fact that she cared so much.

It didn't help that Holly asked frequently when Leland would be coming back to see them. Lauren's vague replies did not satisfy her childish curiosity, and she pursued the point relentlessly, finally suggesting that her mother call him and invite him for dinner.

"Holly, no! That's enough," Lauren snapped, instantly contrite as she saw the tears welling up in Holly's eyes. Gathering the child in her arms, she said, "Honey, I know you like Lee. I do too. But he's a very busy man. I'm sure he'll come to see you as soon as he has a chance. You'll just have to be patient. Can you try to do that?"

"I guess so," she said sorrowfully. "But I hope he comes soon."

Silently, Lauren echoed that wish.

CHAPTER SEVEN

Lauren returned from lunch one afternoon a few days later to find her boss pacing nervously around the waiting room.

"Lauren, thank goodness you're back. I need you in my office right away."

"Of course, Mr. Donovan, I'll be right there," she said, puzzled by his anxious expression. He was usually so calm and unflappable. Gathering up her dictation pad and a pencil, she followed him into his office, trying not to betray her dismay on finding Leland waiting there, his fingers drumming on the desk in irritation.

"Do you suppose we could get started now?" he demanded sharply, giving her a fierce look she felt was totally unwarranted.

"Certainly," she said crisply. "Any time you're ready, Mr. Donovan."

For the next two hours, pausing only long enough

for Lauren to answer the phone and take messages, the two men drew up an agreement on the plans for the Cross office tower. By the time they had finished, her fingers were cramped and her back ached from the tension of trying to keep up. Although she'd had little time to try to absorb the details, it was clear that Leland would have his way with the waterfront property, if the city officials approved the proposal.

"Do you think there are enough votes to get this through without a lot of hassle?" Leland asked anxiously, abandoning his usually confident demeanor.

"I think so, Lee. My sense is that they are reluctant, but pragmatic. They know something like this will have to come to Charleston someday. If that's the case, they might as well go along with your proposal now. They know it's the best they're likely to see."

Leland sighed with relief, but Reed waved a cautioning hand.

"Wait a minute now. Don't go getting your hopes too high. Remember this is an election year. If there is a big hue and cry from the preservationists about those old buildings or from the public about the park land, the whole deal could blow up in our faces. No one will vote for it if there's a chance it could cost them the election."

"How do we avoid a public brawl?" Lee asked wearily. "There will have to be hearings on it."

"Of course. And they will have to be publicized. But perhaps, if it's all handled in a very low-key manner and if it is expedited, it can be over before the press starts to have a heyday with it."

Lauren had an uneasy feeling about what they

74

were planning, but she knew so little about city politics she couldn't pinpoint what bothered her. Finally she decided she'd just leave the two of them to their planning.

"Mr Donovan, if you're through with me, I can get started typing this up," she suggested.

"Fine. But there is one thing I need to warn you about first. You've heard what Lee and I have been saying about the need for this proposal to remain as quiet as possible. I cannot emphasize strongly enough how important it is that what we've drafted remain strictly among the three of us until it goes before the council for a vote. You do understand that, don't you?" he asked.

"Of course. I won't discuss it with anyone."

Two days later, as Lauren was trying to catch up on the correspondence that had been piling up, a young man came into the office looking for her boss.

"I'm sorry, Mr. . . ." she began.

"Hart. Mason Hart."

"I'm sorry, Mr. Hart, but Mr. Donovan is out. Can I help you?"

"Probably even more than Reed Donovan could," he said with an engaging smile. "But I do need to see him. Can I make an appointment?"

"Not this week," Lauren said, glancing at Reed's calendar. "How about next week?"

"If it means I'll get to see you again, I'll come in every day for the next year. How about having a drink with me after work?"

"No, thanks, Mr. Hart. I have to get home after work."

"Is there a husband waiting, who'll clobber me for even asking," he asked in mock horror.

"No. I'm a widow, but I still can't have that drink with you," she said, wondering a bit about her reluctance to accept. With his blond hair, blue eyes, and boyish charm, Mason Hart was an attractive man. He also knew it. That sort of cocky self-assurance could become a little wearing. Or a little dangerous if you made the mistake of taking it too seriously.

For the next week, though, he remained flatteringly persistent. He called to tell her cute little jokes. He stopped by, a bouquet of flowers in hand. He sent her ingratiating notes. In short, he made her feel desirable.

Finally, on Friday, Lauren agreed to have dinner with him. His obvious delight in her acceptance made her feel even more special.

"Wear something gorgeous. I'm going to take you someplace terrific and show you off," he told her.

When he arrived at the house, Holly examined him warily and went promptly back to her room, thus expressing her disapproval. When Lauren and her date were ready to leave, Holly marched stiffly next door to Sue's without a backward glance or even a good-bye for her mother.

"She doesn't seem to be too taken with me," Mason observed wryly.

"I am sorry about that. Holly is usually very friendly," Lauren apologized. "I have no idea what's gotten into her tonight."

"I suppose kids can have a bad day at school, just like we have bad days at the office," he suggested with a shrug. Grinning, he added, "Whatever it is, don't worry about my feelings. As long as her mother finds me fascinating, I can live with Holly's rejection."

He settled Lauren in his bright red, late-model Mustang, then took off as though he were late at the starting gate for the Daytona 500. His choice of car and his driving style reinforced Lauren's analysis of his personality—flashy and a bit reckless. As he roared through the downtown streets, taking corners practically on two wheels, Lauren blanched, clinging to the door to keep from being thrown off her bucket seat. As they crossed the Ashley River and shot off down the open highway, Mason finally noticed her expression of panic.

"I'm sorry. I'm scaring you to death, aren't I," he asked contritely, putting on the brakes. "I forget sometimes that not everyone is in as big a hurry to get places as I am."

Lauren gave a visible sigh of relief. "Thanks. You're right. I'm one of those people who thinks of a car as a lethal weapon that should be kept under tight control. You'd hate being caught behind me on a two-lane road."

He laughed and, after a moment, Lauren relaxed and joined him. "Where are we going?" she asked, trying to pick out familiar landmarks along the road.

"It's an inn that opened a few months ago. It's really quite special. Like you," he said warmly as he turned into a winding driveway marked as the entrance to the Old Town Inn.

The rambling white structure, trimmed in dark green, had a wide porch that stretched all the way across. Rocking chairs, few of them occupied on this cool, late fall evening, were lined up across the porch. The inn was about a half-mile from the main road in a setting of moss-draped oaks and maples with leaves that were turning to orange, red, and yellow shades of the season, which always came a little late to this part of the East Coast. With dusk falling, the temperature was dropping quickly, and smoke pouring out of brick chimneys at either end of the inn indicated that fires were going inside.

"Mason, it looks absolutely marvelous," Lauren enthused, her green eyes sparkling. "It must have been around since Revolutionary War days."

"Hardly that long, though the building itself is probably one hundred fifty years old. It was an old family plantation. About six months ago the heirs decided they couldn't keep up with it. The taxes were spiraling and it needed some major repairs. They decided to turn it into an inn specializing in Southern home-style cooking—fried chicken, corn fritters, that sort of thing. It's caught on quickly, but they've managed to keep it from becoming either overcrowded or rushed. Just wait. I think you'll love it, unless of course, you're partial to discos and wild nightlife."

"Hardly," Lauren said with a laugh. "I think this is exactly my style."

Inside, she caught her breath as she looked around. The entry was wood-paneled and had wide oak floorboards with scattered Oriental carpets in muted tones. Against the highly polished wood floor they were elegant without being intimidating. An antique desk with an embroidered linen mat held the reservations book.

Peeking through the doorway into the main dining

room, she saw that the tables had similar fine linen and were lit by candles in antique pewter holders. Fresh flowers in simple glass vases were on each table. The blazing fireplaces at either end were warmly inviting.

"Mason, you're right. It is absolutely perfect. If the food is only half as terrific as the atmosphere, I'll be in heaven. I'm starved."

The food was superb, the conversation light-hearted, and the after-dinner coffee rich and delicious. It had been such a perfect, undemanding, relaxing evening that Lauren was totally unprepared for the cold shock she felt when she glanced across the room and spotted Leland with a willowy, delicate blonde in an understated, but obviously outrageously expensive dress.

The two of them were engaged in an animated conversation and Leland was laughing heartily at something the woman had said when he looked over and saw Lauren with her escort. His face became stonily impassive and he turned his attention quickly back to his companion, who was clearly dismayed at the sudden change in his mood. Reaching across the table, she put a carefully manicured, dainty hand on top of his and leaned forward to whisper something that brought a trace of a smile to his face.

Lauren could hardly bear the look of intimacy and the touch they exchanged. Suddenly she wanted only to be out of this place, which seemed spoiled, its earlier enchantment destroyed. She wanted to be back at home in front of her own fireplace, wrapped snugly in her old fleece robe, with Holly asleep nearby. Her existence before meeting Leland Cross might have been lonely, but it was uncomplicated and painless. Right now she was feeling a pain so sharp and real, it seemed to make her heart ache.

Mason tried for several minutes to get her attention, then followed the direction of her gaze.

"So that's the impressive Leland Cross, is it?" he asked, ignoring the anguished expression on Lauren's face. "I wonder who that is with him? I heard he was involved with some fashion model from New York. That lady certainly has the looks and class to be a model. Don't you think she looks slightly familiar?"

When Lauren didn't answer, he spoke more sharply. "Lauren?"

"What is it, Mason?"

"I asked if you recognized the woman with Leland Cross."

"No. I don't think so. Mason, would you mind very much if we left now? I'm beginning to get a terrible headache."

"Why don't I just see if they have some aspirin?"

"No. Really. I'd rather leave. Please."

He looked at her oddly, but finally nodded his agreement. "Just let me take care of the bill and we'll be on our way."

Lauren's head was throbbing by the time they stood up to leave. As they started across the room, Mason suggested, "Why don't we stop and speak to Leland Cross? You must know him from work and I'd very much like to meet him."

"No," Lauren said, her voice rising in alarm. "I mean I really don't know him all that well. I don't think it would be a good idea to intrude . . ."

80

But Mason was steering her straight to Leland's table. He rose from his seat at their approach, but his manner was far from welcoming.

He didn't bother to introduce the woman with him, although she was watching the scene with evident interest. Instead, he merely acknowledged Lauren stiffly. "Ms. Mitchell."

"Mr. Cross," she replied, stammering slightly in confusion. She turned pale under his penetrating gaze, but finally managed to add, "This is Mason Hart."

Unaware of the tension in the air or able to ignore it, Mason greeted Leland easily. "It's a pleasure to meet you, sir. I've heard a great deal about you and your office tower. How are the plans coming along?"

"The plans are on schedule," Leland said cryptically. "I hope you two will excuse us now. I see that our dinner is on the way."

Thus dismissed, Lauren turned and fled from the inn, not waiting to see if Mason followed her. Stumbling and twisting her ankle, she was hardly aware of the pain as she ran to the car. Breathless and trembling, she leaned against the side of the car to wait for Mason. When he'd opened the door, she sank gratefully into the plush, comfortable seat.

"Lauren, are you okay?" Mason asked, more puzzled than really concerned, it seemed to Lauren.

"Fine, Mason. It's just that headache."

Weak as the excuse was, it seemed to satisfy him. Nor did he seem to mind that she said little in response to his monologue on the way home. She was too wrapped up in her own misery to notice what he was saying, though she heard Leland's name mentioned a few times.

At the door she apologized for not inviting him in.

"But I did have a lovely evening, Mason," she forced herself to say graciously. "The inn was lovely."

Mason took her remarks at face value, giving her a quick kiss on the cheek before running down the steps. "I'll phone you tomorrow and see how you are," he called back over his shoulder.

After a restless night, Lauren spent all day Saturday trying to get her mind off the scene in the restaurant. The image of Leland and his sophisticated, beautiful date tormented her. Again that night she had nightmares about the two of them wrapped in each other's arms. She awoke shaking and spent hours tossing and turning before finally going back to sleep around dawn.

She was awakened abruptly an hour or so later by the chiming of the doorbell. Groggily pulling on her robe and running her fingers through her mussed hair, she stumbled to the door.

"Who is it?" she called out.

"It's Lee. Open up, Lauren."

Sleepy as she was, she could sense the anger in his tone and for a moment she was frozen into immobility.

"Lauren, damn it, open the door," he ordered.

"Just a minute," she said, ignoring his muttered oath to run to the bathroom and splash some cold water on her face, put on some lipstick and comb her hair properly. By the time she opened the door at last, he was seething.

"What in God's name took you so long?" he snapped as he stormed past her into the living room.

"I am not accustomed to having visitors at the crack of dawn, Mr. Cross. If you want prompt attention on your arrival, then I suggest you call in advance or at least come at a respectable hour," she retorted heatedly.

"Okay. Okay. Forget that. It's not important. What is important is what you're up to. I thought you understood that anything that went on in Reed's office was confidential. How could you possibly do anything so stupid!" He raged while pacing up and down the room, raking his fingers through his hair in a gesture of irritation. When he finally came to stop in front of Lauren, she was shaking with anger.

"I don't know what you are talking about, Leland Cross, and I really am in no mood to play games with you this morning. If you've got something to say, then spit it out and get out of here," she said through clenched teeth.

"You really don't know?" he asked incredulously.

"Know what, Lee?" she replied impatiently.

"Here. Take a look at this," he said, tossing the Sunday paper at her.

There on the front page a bold headline splashed across the top announced CITY LIKELY TO GIVE IN ON OFFICE TOWER. The story quoted sources at City Hall. These unnamed sources revealed that officials were trying to quietly approve the project before preservationists could arm themselves for battle. It went on and on in thoroughly accurate and damning detail.

Now Lauren could understand Leland's rage. This story could do irreparable damage to the project's approval.

"Lee, I'm sorry. This is awful. But what does it have to do with me? I didn't tell anyone about the proposal."

"Not even your new boyfriend?" he snarled sarcastically. "A little pillow talk late at night about what's been happening lately at the office?"

"How dare you!" she said furiously, raising her arm to slap the doubting smirk from his face.

"I wouldn't do that if I were you," he warned, capturing her wrist in a tight grip. His eyes, dark with anger, locked with hers as he spoke slowly and distinctly, each word bitingly cruel in its implication. "There were only three people in that office, Lauren. I haven't talked to anyone and neither has Reed."

"So that leaves me, of course," Lauren said. "Do you both really think so little of my integrity?"

"All right, Lauren," he said, releasing her arm. "You tell me what we should think. Keep in mind that I saw you with the gentleman who wrote the story only two nights ago. I suppose that was just a coincidence?"

"What are you talking about, Lee? I don't know any reporters," she said truthfully, or so she thought.

"That's odd. The name on that story is Mason Hart and I seem to recall your being plenty anxious for me to meet someone by that name Friday night. Or do you suppose there are two Mason Harts in Charleston?"

"Oh, my God," she whispered, sinking down onto

the sofa. "Lee, I swear to you, I had no idea he was a reporter. He never said anything about where he worked. He just came into the office to see Reed and started calling me. I finally agreed to go out with him on Friday."

"And after a few drinks and a fine dinner decided to repay him by spilling your guts to him about the plans for getting the city to approve the office tower?"

"Of course not," she repeated angrily. "I haven't talked to anyone about the project. Or about anything else at work, for that matter."

"Lauren, I find that very difficult to believe with this article staring me in the face in black and white."

"I know. It does look bad," she agreed wearily. "But I'm telling you the truth, Lee. I wouldn't do anything like that. I care too much about my job."

Suddenly the pressure of the morning, of Leland's charges and his lack of faith in her, combined with the pain of having seen him with another woman, all became too much for Lauren. She burst into tears.

Just at that moment Holly came padding into the room in her bright yellow pajamas with the little rabbits all over them. She looked from her sobbing mother to her adored and much-missed Leland, clearly torn about what she should do. Finally she ran to her mother.

"Mommy, why are you crying? Don't cry, please," she begged, trying to comfort Lauren with pats on her shoulder and hugs.

"It's okay, baby. I'm all right," Lauren said, sniffling and trying to regain her composure.

"Why did you make Mommy cry," Holly asked, facing Leland indignantly.

"I didn't mean to, honey," he said guiltily. "It was all a big mistake."

Lauren gazed up at him, her lower lip trembling as she accepted the handkerchief he held out. "You believe that now?" she asked shakily. "That it was a mistake?"

"Yes," he said with conviction. "I'm sorry, Lauren. I guess that's what made me so angry. I wanted to trust you, but I had all that evidence staring me in the face. I had to blame somebody."

"Maybe Mason Hart just made some lucky guesses and asked the right questions in the right places. After all, the mayor and the other officials know this is coming up. They might have let it slip. He is a very aggressive young man."

Leland's glance was possessive, his voice sharp. "Just how aggressive is he?"

Enjoying the moment, Lauren teased. "Very." Then, before he could pursue the point, she headed for the kitchen. "How about some breakfast, you guys? These early-morning brawls wear me out."

Over pancakes, bacon, and eggs, they tried to determine who at City Hall would have had enough information to put Mason Hart on the right track with his story.

"Is that really so important?" Lauren asked after a while. "I mean the story is in the paper now and there's nothing we can do about it. It's accurate, as near as I can tell. The question is how much damage it will do. Do you think it will destroy the chances for the tower?"

"I don't know, Lauren. I really don't. There are a lot of people against it for a lot of different reasons. If they mobilize, it could mean the end for the tower. We'll just have to wait and see."

CHAPTER EIGHT

They didn't have long to wait. The explosion of public anger and outrage took place the following morning, after a night of hastily called meetings and strategy sessions by opponents of the office tower and its location on the harbor.

By midday Lauren was frazzled and nearly frantic. Her phone hadn't stopped ringing since eight A.M., when she'd entered the office for an early meeting with Leland and Reed. Most of the callers were at least polite, but a few, irate over the so-called coverup by city officials, vented their feelings in very explicit terms. There was even a threat of violence and, while Lauren was sure it was made in the heat of the moment and was not serious, she had reported it to the police anyway.

Reed's morning had been equally harried. While Lauren had fended off the callers, he had had to deal with the mayor and other city officials who were demanding an explanation of how the story had leaked out.

"Enough of this," he declared, coming out of his office about two o'clock. Taking Lauren's phone off the hook, he ordered her to go out for some lunch.

"But I can't leave you alone here. It's a madhouse."

"I'll manage. Now get moving. If you don't take a break for a few minutes, you're liable to fall apart on me. Besides, I can use a sandwich too. You can bring one back when you come."

Lauren looked skeptical.

"Go," he insisted. "Before I change my mind. And don't forget the ketchup for my hamburger."

Gratefully Lauren escaped, knowing that Reed was right, that a few minutes away from her desk would make the rest of the afternoon bearable. Seated in a booth at the sandwich shop in the next block, she ordered a chicken salad sandwich and a cup of coffee. While she waited for it to come, she massaged the back of her neck and closed her eyes. Suddenly her hands were pushed aside and a strong, masculine touch took over the task, kneading away the knots of tension. Instinctively she knew it was Leland, though he didn't say a word until he'd stopped his massage and seated himself across from her.

"This has been the rottenest day of my career," he admitted wearily, his voice drained of its usual combative spirit.

"I have been described as greedy, grasping, a Yankee carpetbagger, and a lot of things I can't even repeat. The residents of Charleston, it's safe to say, are not taking this well. They seem to welcome the

Cross office tower with all the warmth they felt for the Union soldiers. They're certainly arming for the same sort of battle."

Slumped down across from her, his collar open, his tie askew, he was the picture of dejection. Noticing Lauren's pitying look, he managed a smile.

"Don't look so glum, Lauren. This'll pass. I've weathered other storms in other cities."

"I know, but I still feel responsible."

"I thought we'd decided this wasn't your fault. I'd still like to know where Hart did get his information, though," Leland said, reaching over and taking half of Lauren's sandwich.

"Get your own, you thief," she teased, trying to snatch it back. But he had already wolfed down most of it and the rest he held away from her reach.

"I'll buy you dessert instead," he replied, calling the waitress over to bring more coffee and a couple of pieces of homemade apple pie.

When they'd finished the pie, Lauren picked up Reed's hamburger and they walked back to the office together. Again, they were greeted with chaos. Reed had put the phones back on the hook and was trying to cope with all the lines. He was talking on one, had another on hold, and two more were ringing.

Lauren took care of the calls and was about to go back to her own office when Reed stopped her.

"Lauren, this one's for you. Why don't you take it here," he said in an odd tone of command.

She gave him a puzzled look as she took the receiver. "Hello. This is Lauren Mitchell. May I help you?" she asked politely. Listening to the reply, her face became flushed and her eyes flashed angrily.

Reed watched her reaction closely and Leland eyed them both curiously.

"Why, you . . . you," she sputtered, clinging to the phone when Leland tried to yank it from her hand.

"If it's an obscene call, let me handle it," he hissed sharply. Lauren shook her head, mouthing, "It's not."

Aloud she said, "How dare you call here, Mr. Hart! After what you've done, why would you think I'd ever want to see you or even speak to you again?"

Again Leland tried to snatch the phone away, frantically signaling to her. She put Mason Hart on hold and turned to Leland.

"What on earth is wrong with you?"

"Does he want to see you again?" he asked. At her nod, he continued, "Then see him."

"Are you out of your mind?" Lauren's tone emphasized her confusion about his request. Even Reed looked startled at the suggestion.

"See him, Lauren," Leland repeated. "I want you to try to find out where he got his information."

"But, Lee, I don't want to see him again. Besides, he is obviously very clever and he's not about to tell me anything about his sources."

"Please, Lauren. Just do it. I think you can find a way to make him talk. Use a little of that charm on him," he said, his tone suggestively teasing.

Lauren was indignant. "Lee, I can't do that."

"Sure you can. Just look at the effect you've had on me and I'm a very wary bachelor." He gave her his most beguiling grin. "Honey, it's important. Really."

"Oh, all right," she said. "But I don't like it."

"I don't want you to like it," he said pointedly.

Lauren went back to Mason Hart, apologizing for the interruption and managing to maneuver an invitation for a drink after work.

As she hung up she gave Leland a wry look. "It's a good thing our Mr. Hart has a large ego. He seemed completely willing to overlook my earlier hostility and assume I had somehow come to my senses about his irresistible charms. Why didn't I notice the other night what a disgustingly singleminded man he is?"

"Probably because you were too busy shooting daggers at Gloria," Leland suggested lightly.

"Gloria?"

"Yes. Gloria Trudeau. The young woman at my table who seemed to be spoiling your meal."

"Leland Cross, your ego is even larger than Mason Hart's. What makes you think I even noticed you, much less your companion?" Lauren's heated response drew an amused glance from Reed and Leland.

"Lauren, don't ever get into a poker game. Your face is easier to read than a grade-school primer," Leland said, laughing as he waved good-bye to Reed and headed for the door.

"Why you smug, arrogant, impossible . . ." Lauren shouted after him, stopping as Leland softly closed the door behind him.

Hours later, as Lauren waited in a nearby restaurant for Mason Hart, she thought about what Leland had said. It was true. She'd never been a particularly good liar. She wondered now how she was going to pull off this meeting. Surely Mason would see right

93

through her civil facade and what would she do then?

"Hi, lovely." He greeted her breezily, interrupting her worrying. "I'm glad you changed your mind."

Lauren smiled wanly, hoping he wouldn't ask why she'd agreed to meet him. He didn't. Instead, he said, "You look worn to a frazzle. Rough day at the office?"

His concern sounded genuine, but she couldn't trust him, not after his deception.

"No rougher than usual," she said at last.

"Funny. I would have thought you'd have been besieged by phone calls today."

Lauren gave him a speculative look, trying to guess what he was after this time. She was determined not to give him any more ammunition for the crusade he was obviously mounting. There was an uncomfortable silence as she debated what approach she should take with him. When she finally spoke, her tone was curt.

"Mason, let's stop fencing. I saw the story. I know you're a reporter, something I wish I'd known before we ever went out last week."

"Would it have made a difference?"

"It might have, particularly if I'd known what story you were working on. Now that I do know, I want to make it clear that I have no intention of discussing my work with you. If you have any questions about what goes on in the city planning director's office, call Reed Donovan."

"You really are angry, aren't you?" he said with unmistakable surprise. "Why?"

"Because you were not open with me. As a result,

when that story came out, some people jumped to a fairly natural conclusion that I was the one who gave you the information. It put me in a very awkward position with some people I like and respect."

"Such as Leland Cross?" The question was loaded with meaning and he gave her a penetrating glance as he waited for her reply.

"He's one of them. Reed Donovan is another. He gave me a job at a time when I really needed one. He had faith in me and now I think that faith is shaken just a little bit."

"But that's not your fault. You didn't give me any information. Your name never appeared anywhere in connection with the article."

Lauren gave a short, derisive laugh. "Do you really think the absence of my name made any difference, when we were seen together just two days before the article appeared? In fact, it was almost as though you went out of your way to make sure we were seen by Leland Cross. Who were you trying to protect, Mason?"

"Come on, Lauren. You don't really expect me to answer that. A good reporter never reveals his sources. Not even to someone as beautiful as you."

Lauren ignored the compliment, which was slightly too glib. "Tell me, Mason," she said, not even trying to keep the sarcasm from her voice, "are you protecting your sources again tonight?"

"What do you mean?"

"Isn't it obvious? Are you seeing me tonight so your source will be in the clear when your next story breaks?"

He looked at her incredulously. "You can't be serious. I called because I enjoy your company."

"Somehow I'm finding that difficult to believe," she said skeptically.

To Lauren's surprise, Mason actually seemed hurt by her attitude. His tone was defensive when he tried to explain his actions.

"If you recall our evening in any detail, Lauren, you'll remember that I never once tried to question you about your job. Sure, I maneuvered that introduction to Leland Cross. But only after he turned up there coincidentally. I had no idea he'd be at the inn for dinner. Since he was, I figured I might as well get our meeting out of the way. Sooner or later I will have to interview him."

"Why not before you ran that article? Isn't the usual journalistic practice to get both sides of the story before you go into print," Lauren probed.

Mason remained unflustered by her question. "It depends on the story. Sometimes it's just as well to get the issue out in the open first and then let the people involved start their namecalling afterward."

"Once it's too late, no doubt."

The harshness of her comment hit its mark. After a moment's discomfort, Mason took aim right back at her. "Why is this so important to you, Lauren? I'm sure you've had no real trouble clearing up whatever problems the story might have caused you at first. So what's your interest now? Leland Cross? Is there something between the two of you?"

"Of course not," she denied heatedly. "I just hate to see this blown out of all proportion in the paper."

Mason shook his head in exasperation. "Lauren, I

did not blow anything out of proportion. Was there anything inaccurate in that story?"

"No, but it all looked so . . . so underhanded and that's not the way it was at all."

"Maybe not. But if everything really was all proper, why the effort to keep it quiet?"

"Because—" Lauren paused, certain that anything she could say would only make matters worse.

"Because your boss, Leland Cross, the mayor, and the council hoped they could push it through without attracting any attention. Don't you think the people of Charleston have a right to know that an office tower that could change the face of this city is about to be approved? And that the building might very well go on waterfront land that had been intended as a park?"

"I suppose so," she said hesitantly. "I guess I never thought of it that way."

"Well, you should. You're one of those people who might be robbed of a park. You and your little girl. Don't you care about that at all?"

"Of course, I do."

"Well, all I'm saying is that the people who care should have a chance to do something about it, that they shouldn't find out after it's too late. It's my job to see that doesn't happen."

Lauren was beginning to see his point of view. He had put into words some of those doubts she had had that day in Reed's office when the proposal had been drawn up.

Mason sensed that he was beginning to make an impression and he pushed his advantage.

"Lauren, I know you feel a certain loyalty to your

boss. I admire you for that. But that doesn't mean that you have to be an unthinking cog in the machinery at City Hall. What those men were trying to do was wrong. I don't expect you to admit that for the record, but you should at least consider the possibility that they made a mistake in judgment."

Suddenly she wanted to be alone—someplace where she could think all of this through. It was hard for her to conceive of Reed Donovan doing anything really wrong, at least intentionally. Nor was she willing to admit that Leland, in a ruthless attempt to get his way, had tried to push through a shady deal. But she couldn't deny that Mason had made a convincing case against them. Perhaps he had only been trying to do his job as a reporter and she had just been an innocent victim in it all. She studied him as he waited for her response, deciding that she'd been correct when she'd described him to Leland as singleminded. Only she was discovering that his singlemindedness might indeed be a virtue rather than the flaw she'd implied.

"I've got to go," she announced abruptly, standing up. She started toward the door, then came back. "I will think about what you've said."

"That's all I ask," he said.

CHAPTER NINE

Lauren drove around after leaving Mason, winding up along the waterfront near the site where Leland wanted to build his office tower. Sitting in her car, she tried to sort out her thoughts about what he and the city officials had tried to do, Mason's role in revealing it, and her own relationship to Leland, which was becoming more and more complicated by her growing attraction to him.

A part of her was undeniably drawn to his strength and his power, his certainty about what he wanted from life. But, she reminded herself, there was a determination that bordered on ruthlessness in him, a cold edge of steel to his actions that was almost frightening. Had she not seen another side to his personality, his tenderness in passion, his gentle sensitivity to Holly, Lauren could not possibly have fallen in love with him. And that, she admitted at last, was exactly what she had done—fallen in love, hopelessly, passionately, heart-shatteringly.

What bothered her more than anything was knowing that she wanted him so much that she would go to him on his terms. Her love for him was so overpowering that she knew it was useless to try to deny it any longer. She wanted to feel his arms around her, to feel that unending strength protecting her and stirring her to dizzying heights.

That's no good, she argued with herself, knowing that she'd already lost the argument. Her thoughts tumbled in kaleidoscopic fashion, forming image after image of Leland, his gray eyes glinting with amusement.

That image was still taunting her when she arrived at Sue's to pick up Holly.

"She's in the living room, and wait until you see the gorgeous creature who's with her," Sue said, casting her an envious glance.

"Who?"

"Says his name's Lee and that he's a pal of Holly's. From the way she flew into his arms, I gathered he wasn't lying or trying to kidnap her."

At Lauren's look of dismay, Sue tried to reassure her. "Hey, don't look so worried. Just in case he wasn't what he claimed, I haven't taken my eyes off of him. Which," she added with a grin, "wasn't all that painful."

Lauren had to laugh at Sue's pretense of lechery. Her attractive twenty-eight-year-old neighbor hadn't given so much as a passing glance at another man in the ten years she'd been married to her high school sweetheart.

"Maybe I should get the kids and go on home so you can be alone with him," Lauren offered mischievously.

"Hey, great," Sue agreed after a moment's thought. "Just be sure to come back in time to pick up the pieces after Jeff breaks every dish in the house. He tends to overreact when he finds strange men in our bedroom."

"Oh? Has he found many?"

"Fourteen just last week," Sue said, causing them both to dissolve into giggles, like a couple of teen-aged conspirators.

They were still laughing as they walked into the living room, where Leland was stretched out on the floor, Holly in the crook of one arm, David, Sue's son, in the other.

He was so totally absorbed in reading the children a story about pirates that he didn't even notice when Lauren and Sue entered. Lauren noted that he seemed to be thoroughly enjoying the part about the bad guys being forced to walk the plank. As he rumbled the pirate's orders in his deep voice, she closed her eyes and for a minute she could envision him as a daring soldier of fortune. His expression was fierce, his hair an unruly dark tangle, his complexion the dark tan of a man who'd been at sea.

When the story ended, in the happily-ever-after style of most storybooks, Lauren joined the children in their applause.

"Not bad for a novice," she teased.

"Lady, I'm no novice," he responded indignantly. "In fact, if you stick around, you'll discover I've all sorts of skills we haven't tested yet."

Lauren blushed furiously and turned her attention to Holly to cover her confusion. "Hey, kiddo, don't you even have a kiss for your mother?"

"Sure," Holly said, bounding over to give her a kiss that was sticky from the grape lollipop she'd been licking. "Guess what, Mommy? Lee brought things for dinner. He said he'd read to me some more while you cook."

"Is that so?" Lauren asked, giving him an impish look. "How come I can't read to you while he cooks, if he's the one who wants dinner?"

Holly studied her mother and Leland carefully, pondering the question, then announced, "I don't think Lee can cook, Mommy."

"Oh, yes, I can, you little monster, and just to prove it, I will fix dinner. You will both be awed and amazed at my culinary skills."

"We'll see. Just in case, maybe I ought to order a pizza," Lauren suggested.

"Don't do that," Sue said. "You can all come back here if he burns everything."

"Enough of that kind of talk, ladies. I intend to exact a heavy payment for those slanderous remarks," he said, giving Lauren a meaningful look. "Sue, thank you again for taking me in and letting me wait here for Lauren."

"Any time," she offered. "Just give me time to shoo Jeff out the back door."

An hour later, to Lauren's absolute amazement, Leland made good on his promise. After banishing her from the kitchen, he'd baked potatoes, tossed a salad, and broiled three steaks to medium-rare perfection. He'd even found her crystal wineglasses for the Cabernet-Sauvignon he'd brought along.

"I'm impressed," she conceded between bites. "What are you fixing tomorrow night?"

"Don't get greedy, my pet," he warned, his tone mellowing when he looked at Holly, who was nearly asleep in her chair. "Looks as though I'm about to lose part of my audience."

"If you don't mind taking her to bed, I'll clear up in here," Lauren said, beginning to stack the dishes on a tray. Leland was back in time to help dry the last of the dishes and then together they went to sit on the sofa in front of the fire.

When they were settled at opposite ends of the sofa, Lauren with her legs tucked under her, Leland asked, "Well, tell me. What happened with Mason Hart?"

"So that's what this is all about," she said with mock dismay. "And here I thought you'd come over just for the pleasure of our company."

"Lauren," he warned ominously, "don't test me."

"Okay. Okay. Actually, I learned absolutely nothing from Mason. He merely gave me a lecture on protecting sources and on the public's right to know. I must admit I thought he had a point on both counts," she added as an afterthought.

"You what?" Leland shouted, leaping to his feet, anger etched in his features. "You think that article was fair? That article has pretty nearly ruined my chances for getting approval for the office tower. Do you realize what a building like that could mean for Charleston's future?"

"And for yours," Lauren suggested quietly.

The silence that followed her comment was deafening. When Leland looked at her at last, it was as though he faced a traitor. Still, he spoke softly and his voice held no rancor.

"Yes. And for mine. Lauren, I care about my work. I am not an ogre out to destroy this town's charm. I believe that the tower is well designed and that it belongs exactly where I want to put it, not three blocks away or even a block away."

"Why does it have to go there? I suspect it's only because you are too darn stubborn to admit that another site might be just as effective," Lauren challenged.

"Lauren, you don't know what you're talking about."

"Oh?" Her tone was heavy with sarcasm. "I think I do. You haven't given me one good reason why that tower can't be built inland. The people who rent there aren't going to be taking deliveries by ship, for heaven's sake.

"Sure, all that glass and steel would look great shimmering in a giant reflection on the water. And, of course, the view would be wonderful for the tenants. But wouldn't the view be just as spectacular if the building were across the street? Especially if the land in between is turned into a park filled with trees and flowers?"

Lauren's face was filled with excitement as she envisioned what it could be like. She knew that Leland remained unconvinced, and she was determined to reach him with logic, rather than sheer sentiment.

"Lee, I know you feel that your building won't make that big a difference to what happens along the waterfront, that there will still be plenty of land left for parks. But, don't you see? With your tower there, that land will be more attractive to other developers. They'll want a piece here, then a few lots there, and pretty soon there won't be a sliver of waterfront left.

"You say you don't want to destroy Charleston's waterfront. Maybe not. But you sure as heck want to exploit it."

Leland looked as though she had slapped him.

"Do you really believe that?" he asked, stunned by her vehemence.

"I think your determination to get your own way might have clouded your thinking. You're an intelligent man, Lee. And, contrary to what some people seem to believe, I don't think you're a greedy one. So please, just think this through."

"Why do you care so much?"

"I suppose I'm thinking about Holly and what it will be like for her in ten or fifteen years if the city is nothing but concrete and every building with any history attached to it has been leveled in the name of progress. I love the waterfront. I spent some of my happiest hours as a teen-ager walking along the Battery, looking out to sea. As the pace of living gets more and more frantic, even here, I think it will be important for people to have parks, to have places that are soothing for the soul.

"As for those landmarks you want to knock down, well, maybe those couple of buildings aren't all that important, but once you start tearing down any part of the past, you're taking away something that's irreplaceable."

For a moment, she felt embarrassed. "Does that sound too sentimental or corny?"

"A little, perhaps, but they're nice thoughts just the same," he said gently, sitting beside her and drawing her into his arms. He held her for several minutes without speaking, then drew back to gaze into her eyes.

"You know, Ms. Mitchell, I think I feel the same way about you that you feel about those green spaces. You are very soothing for my soul."

He kissed her then, a slow, tantalizing kiss that set Lauren's pulse racing. Pulling away, he traced her still-tingling lips with his fingertips, smiling as a shudder shook her body.

His eyes seemed to burn with an intense longing as he told her huskily, "Kissing you, on the other hand, is definitely not soothing. Quite the contrary, in fact."

Again he lowered his mouth to hers and that gentle contact ignited a flame of passion between them. Lauren clung to him, her body weak with longing and desire.

His hands moved gently over her shoulders, stroking and caressing. When they reached her already-throbbing breasts, the chill of his fingers through the thin silk of her blouse made her nipples respond immediately, sending waves of pleasant sensations coursing through her body.

Her own hands, tentatively at first, massaged the rippling muscles of his back, then moved to his chest. Her fingers traced the burning skin visible above the open collar of his shirt, then unbuttoned the remain-

106

ing buttons until his entire chest was bared to her trembling touch.

Hesitantly Lauren raised her eyes to meet Leland's, which revealed a naked hunger equal to her own. Assuming the unfamiliar role of aggressor, she explored his body with her hands, sprinkling kisses on his lips, his eyes, his shoulders, and the hair-rough expanse of his chest. Never before had she felt so free and uninhibited, her own passion mounting as she saw the effect her lovemaking was having on him. His breathing was ragged as he pulled her at last into a demanding embrace.

"I want you, Lauren. My God, how I want you," he murmured hungrily as he removed her clothing piece by piece, branding her skin with a touch of fire that silenced all the warning bells in her mind. Her body had a mind of its own tonight, and it was perfectly attuned to Leland's. She would not deny him this one night, no matter the consequences.

When the last bit of lacy fabric had been removed, Lauren lay on the sofa, her body bathed in the warm glow of the fire. Leland stood for a moment reveling in her beauty, his eyes alight with pleasure and desire. Just as he lowered himself beside her, whispering endearments as she moaned and drew closer to him, a tiny voice, filled with fear, interrupted their moment of ecstasy.

"Mommy! Mommy!" Holly screamed, her terror bringing Lauren instantly to her feet, a stricken expression on her face. Leland, his own face reflecting a mixture of guilt and concern, pushed her back.

"You can't go like that, honey. Let me go. I'll see

107

what's wrong with her. It's probably just a bad dream."

As soon as he had gone, Lauren ran upstairs to her own room and got a robe. Clutching it around her, she went back to the living room, where she sat trembling until Leland returned.

"Is she all right?" she asked anxiously.

"It was nothing. Just a nightmare. She went right back to sleep," he said, slumping down in a chair facing Lauren.

The moment of magic between them was lost. In its wake Lauren felt confused and guilty. This was no way to live, stealing momentary thrills which would fade by morning. True, she loved Leland. But to him, she was one of many women and that was not good enough for her.

Unsure of how to confront the issue, she almost decided to let it pass for now. Somehow she would see to it that it wasn't repeated. Just when she would have abandoned any idea of a confrontation, she recalled a bit of advice Elsie Cates had given her when they'd talked about her long and happy marriage. Elsie had emphasized the importance of communicating, no matter how painful.

Lauren forced herself to speak. "Lee, we've got to talk about what happened tonight. It can't happen again."

"If you mean this feeling of guilt, I agree."

"No, I mean our making love," Lauren said, her voice barely above a whisper.

"Honey, there's no way that won't happen again. I'm a virile, red-blooded male. You are an attractive woman. The chemistry between us is not going to go away just because we might like it to."

"We don't have to give in to it," Lauren insisted. "We're adults, pretty strong-willed adults at that."

"Is that what you want? Honestly, Lauren," he demanded harshly.

Lauren's eyes were filled with torment as she said shakily, "I don't know what I want anymore. But I do know I don't like feeling cheap or dirty, and that's how I feel right now."

"Because of Holly, right?" he asked perceptively.

"That's part of it, I guess."

"Then I have a solution."

"So do I. We avoid situations like tonight, romantic little settings, cozy chats by the fire."

"No," Leland said sharply, his tone taking her aback with its forcefulness. "We get married. As soon as possible."

Lauren's shock at his proposal was genuine. Unable to speak, she merely sat and stared at him.

"In fact," he continued, ignoring her silence or taking it for assent, "you can ask Sue to look after Holly for a few days and we'll fly to Maryland, get married there tomorrow, and then go on to New York. I have some business to take care of there anyway."

His tone was as matter-of-fact as if he'd been arranging for delivery of the evening paper. There was no hint of emotion in his voice, nothing to convince Lauren that he really cared.

"But . . . but I thought you didn't want to get married," she said haltingly.

"I've changed my mind," he said easily. "Speak to

Sue first thing in the morning and I'll arrange things with Reed. We can leave tomorrow afternoon."

"What about Holly?"

"I told you. Get Sue to look after her."

"No. I mean how do you feel about . . . about raising another man's child?"

For a moment he looked at her as though she'd lost her mind.

"Lauren, I love Holly. Surely you can see that. I'd adopt her in a minute if that's what you wanted. Now will you please stop being ridiculous and make the arrangements?"

Still, she hedged.

"I can't take time off from work now. I just started," she said, aware that the argument was absurd when measured against a marriage that would change her life.

Leland tried to be patient. "I'm sure Elsie Cates can fill in for you for a few days. If necessary, *I'll* call her. Now then, any more arguments?"

Only one, Lauren thought, but she could not bring herself to voice it, even though it was the most critical of all. She already knew the answer: He did not love her. But, perhaps, in time, his desire would change to real love.

Seeing the look of determination in his eyes, she gave in.

"All right, Lee," she said at last. "I'll marry you."

In her heart, where fear and joy were at war, she prayed she was doing the right thing.

CHAPTER TEN

Lauren awoke in the morning certain that she had only dreamed Leland's proposal, that her happiness was an illusion that would drift away on the morning breeze. She was afraid to speak to Sue, as Leland had suggested, sure that in the cold light of day, he would change his mind and cling to his bachelorhood.

She followed her normal routine as closely as possible, mechanically fixing Holly's breakfast, dropping her off at school, and then going to the office. She had barely hung up her jacket and taken the cover off of her typewriter when Elsie Cates called.

"Lauren, honey, I can't tell you how excited I am. I just knew that you and Lee were perfect for each other, but I didn't dare to hope the two of you would figure it out for yourselves so soon."

Lauren was speechless with surprise, but it hardly mattered. Elsie was perfectly capable of filling the conversational gaps. "Don't you worry about a thing here. I'll be glad to come in for a few days. In fact, I can be there by noon today, so you can have some time to shop and get packed."

When Elsie finally paused for breath, Lauren asked, "How did you find out?" She had little doubt about the answer.

"Why, Lee called me not fifteen minutes ago and told me. He wanted to be sure I'd be able to fill in for you so he could reassure Reed."

"You mean he's told Mr. Donovan already too?" she asked a little breathlessly as she realized that Leland was already beginning his mastery of her life.

"I suppose so. He told me he was about to call him. Lauren, is everything all right? You sound a little funny."

Lauren gave a shaky laugh. "I'm fine, Elsie. Just a little breathless, I guess. I'm not used to things moving so fast. I feel as though I just discovered I'm on a roller coaster when I thought I'd bought a ticket for a merry-go-round."

"Well, don't you worry your pretty little head about anything. Leland Cross is a man who knows exactly what he wants and how to get it. He'll take care of things from now on."

"So I see," Lauren said, her voice filled with irony. "I only hope he'll let me decide what to wear to the wedding."

She looked up in time to see Leland coming through the door, his expression turning to a scowl as he caught sight of her.

"Elsie, I've got to go now. The general has arrived with my next batch of orders, judging from the look on his face. Thanks for everything. I'll see you a little later."

"What was that comment about orders?" he asked, perching on the edge of her desk.

"Just a reference to your busy morning, Mr. Cross. Half the town seems to know more about our wedding plans than I do."

"What's that supposed to mean? I merely took care of a couple of details, exactly as I told you I would last night. By the way, what the devil are you doing in here? Shouldn't you be home getting ready to leave?"

"Perhaps if I knew precisely what our timetable was, I could pace myself accordingly," she said curtly.

"Lauren, what on earth is the matter with you? I thought you wanted this marriage. Have you changed your mind?"

She sighed and shook her head. "No. I haven't changed my mind. I suppose the last few months of being on my own have made me more independent than I realized. I'm not sure I want someone to just walk in and take over my life again."

"Honey, this is no time to get into a discussion about your independence. I have no intention of trying to run your life. I'm just trying to get this wedding together on schedule. After that you can have all the freedom you want to make your own decisions."

"But it's all happening so fast, Lee. Why do we have to get married today, for instance?"

"Why not get it over with? I have to go to New

113

York anyway, and that'll give us a honeymoon of sorts. It just seems like the logical time."

"You sound like one of those efficiency experts they hire to eliminate wasted motions," Lauren said sarcastically.

Her remark only increased his impatience. "What do you want me to sound like? Some bloody romantic fool?"

Lauren had to bite her tongue to keep from shouting, "Yes, damn it, that's exactly what I want." She knew better than to expect a little romance and tenderness. He was marrying her for reasons she had yet to fully analyze, but certainly not for love. She'd have to be content with the legality of being his wife and hope that proximity would do the rest.

Before they could continue their discussion, which was threatening to become heated despite Lauren's best intentions, Reed came striding in. He gave Lauren an approving smile and shook Leland's hand heartily.

"Congratulations, young man. I never thought I'd live to see the day you got caught, but I should have known Lauren could do it. She's a very talented woman. Beautiful too, as I'm sure you've noticed."

"Oh, I've noticed," Leland said wryly, his eyes traveling possessively over her body.

"Lauren, if this man gives you the slightest bit of trouble, you just let me know about it. I'll see to it that the city tables any action on his building until he shapes up and treats you right."

Lauren laughed. "Please, don't do that, Mr. Donovan," she begged, in mock horror. "You know how impossible he is when he doesn't get his way."

114

"So do you, my dear. That's why I was so surprised to hear you'd agreed to marry him. Are you sure you want to let yourself in for a lifetime with this man?"

Lauren paused, as though seriously pondering the question. "Now that you mention it . . ." she began, only to be cut off in mid-sentence, as Leland leaned down and covered her lips with his own.

When the kiss ended, Lauren said breathlessly, "On the other hand, he is very persuasive."

Reed chuckled as he shook Leland's hand again. "Well, I wish you two the very best. I only wish we could be there for the wedding. Elsie Cates is convinced she's responsible for this match and she hates to miss a wedding she's had a hand in arranging."

"She can console herself that her presence in here is allowing Lauren to have a honeymoon," Leland offered. "Seriously, Reed, I appreciate your understanding in all this. I'll deliver your secretary safely back here in a few days."

"Take your time. Elsie and I will manage," he said, leaving them alone.

After telling her what time he would pick her up to make their flight, Leland left without so much as a farewell kiss. Lauren stared after him, once more assailed by doubts and uncertainty. Fortunately, she thought, there was little time for her to indulge her feelings of panic. She had to talk to Sue about keeping Holly, tell Holly what was happening, and pack. She wished there were time to find something really special for the trip, a daring negligee or an elegant dress.

She was sitting at her desk daydreaming when

115

Elsie arrived promptly at noon to take over for her. She came in bearing a huge box wrapped in silver foil with a fancy white bow. She handed it to Lauren.

"Elsie, what have you done?" she asked, getting up to give the woman an impulsive kiss.

"Oh, it's just a little something. I knew you wouldn't have much time to do anything today, so I just decided to do a little shopping for you."

Excitedly, Lauren unwrapped the package, gasping with pleasure as she drew out a filmy turquoise nightgown and matching robe. Tailored in style, with only the slightest edging of lace, the gown was cut flatteringly low on top and had slits clear to mid-thigh on the sides. It was very sophisticated, very feminine, and exceptionally sexy.

"Oh, Elsie, it's just perfect," she said, tears in her eyes as she hugged her friend. "I love it."

"Every bride wants something wonderful to wear on her wedding night," Elsie said with a conspiratorial wink. "Now you just get on out of here and get ready. Don't keep that man of yours waiting."

"Oh, Elsie, what can I ever do to thank you?"

"You can be happy. That's all the thanks I want."

A few hours later, standing before a justice of the peace and his beaming wife in a tiny Maryland town, Lauren wondered if happiness was, in fact, within her reach. Certainly, the justice of the peace seemed to find nothing odd in this hurried ceremony. No doubt he'd performed hundreds just like it, a tape recording of the wedding march playing in the background while his wife snapped pictures with an instant camera for an additional three-dollar fee.

As the words of the brief civil service began, Lauren's mind drifted back to another wedding. She could not recall feeling the same mixture of hope, anticipation, and panic as she and Doug had exchanged vows. Now she was clutching her bouquet of daisies and white roses so tightly she was sure the flowers would wilt before the final "I do."

As though from a long distance away, she heard Leland's promise to love and cherish her. Then it was her turn and her voice echoed in her ears as she swore to be Leland's "until death do us part." When, at last, the justice of the peace pronounced them man and wife, Leland's fleeting kiss did little to banish the feeling of unreality that surrounded Lauren. In a daze, she stood by as he paid the official and his wife, tucked the marriage certificate into his pocket along with the snapshots of the ceremony, and agreed to drink a toast to their happiness.

As the four of them sipped their champagne, Lauren tried to find some way to convince herself that this was her wedding day. The bouquet, her blue silk dress, the thin gold band on her left hand—none of it made any sense. Less than twenty-four hours earlier she had been a single mother, facing the world alone. She had not even been engaged. Now here she was, married to a man she barely knew, hundreds of miles from home. What in God's name had she been thinking of? Her eyes lifted to meet Leland's gaze. He must have seen the panic in them, because instantly he began steering her out the door and into the waiting taxi.

When they were on their way back to the Washington airport to catch a shuttle flight to New York, he took her trembling hand in his.

"Having a case of the jitters, Lauren?"

Unable to speak for fear that the unshed tears would spill down her face, Lauren merely nodded.

"What about me?" he teased. "At least you've been through this before. I'm a first-timer."

She gave him a shaky smile. "Don't try to tell me you're nervous, Leland Cross. You've finalized bigger deals than this one."

"See there. Your spirit's coming back already," he said, giving her a squeeze. "By the way, is that how you see this? As a deal?"

"Isn't it?"

"Not to me, it isn't. When a business proposition goes sour, I can always buy my way out of it. I've no intention of buying my way out of this marriage. Like the man said, it's for keeps, till death do us part."

His comment, made with icy determination, was hardly a declaration of undying love, but at least it reassured Lauren that he intended to make their marriage work. As though reading her thoughts, he told her, "It took me a long time to decide to marry, Lauren. Now that I have, I intend to see to it that it's more than the shallow arrangement my father had with my mother."

During the quick flight to New York, Lauren stemmed the tide of her growing nervousness by repeating his vow over and over in her mind. She was still thinking about it when they landed at La-Guardia.

"Honey, you wait here while I get the luggage," he

118

said, positioning her near the exit. When he returned a few minutes later, a burly man with reddish hair and a wide smile was with him.

"You must be the new missus," he said, taking Lauren's hand. "I'm Jim O'Donovan. I work for Mr. Cross. My wife's the housekeeper. We sure are glad about the news, ma'am. We'd about given up on marrying this one off."

Leland smiled at the man's exuberance.

"Don't mind Jim, Lauren. He and Bridie have been with me so long, they think I'm their son. Bridie's the only person in the world who can tell me what to do and get away with it."

"Perhaps she'll teach me her techniques," Lauren said, laughing at Leland's look of mock horror.

"Looks to me like you've met your match, boss."

As they drove into the city, Jim weaving through the heavy traffic with the skill and daring of long experience, Lauren's doubts fled, to be replaced by sheer joy at the spectacle around her. For all her previously expressed love of open spaces, the concrete jungle that was New York had an excitement about it that was unmistakable. The city throbbed with activity and life.

When the car pulled up in front of a high-rise building on a fashionable street on the East Side, Lauren was surprised. Even though she'd heard what Jim had said about his wife being Leland's housekeeper, it apparently hadn't registered that he had his own place. Lauren had been expecting just a small suite of rooms in a hotel.

Upstairs on the thirty-first floor, with the city lights spread out below, Bridie was waiting for them,

119

her plump arms open wide to welcome Lauren with a warm embrace.

"Sure and you're a wee slip of a lass," she clucked. "But you're a beauty all right. Looks as though my lad has done right well for himself."

Lauren blushed at the compliment.

"Now you come with me, young lady, and I'll show you to your room. You must be wantin' to freshen up a bit after your long day."

Bridie bustled down the hallway, pointing out a guest room and a den along the way to the master bedroom, a huge room decorated in masculine taste —the earth tones of the carpet, drapes, and spread, brightened with green and orange accents. A king-size bed, which brought a tingling sensation to the pit of Lauren's stomach, dominated the room.

"You just settle in here, little Laurie, and my Jim will be along in a minute with your bags. I've got dinner warming in the oven and soon as I get it on the table we'll be gettin' along and leavin' you two alone."

"Thank you, Bridie," Lauren said, sinking down gratefully into an overstuffed chair covered in a durable tweed fabric with tiny flecks of orange, brown, and green on a beige background. She kicked off her shoes and propped her feet up on an ottoman, allowing her eyelids to drift shut for just a minute.

She must have fallen into a deep sleep almost instantly, exhausted by the events of the past day. The next thing she knew Leland's caressing touch on her shoulders was blending with a dream she was having. When she awoke fully, her body was already responding to the insistent probing of his expert fingers.

"Hi, sleeping beauty," he murmured softly, nuzzling her throat and leaving a trail of kisses along the sensitive hollows at the base of her neck. Instantly a warm glow spread through her body, as her ardency flamed to match his.

"You know," he whispered into her ear, his hands continuing their merciless pattern of torment, "if we don't get in there and eat Bridie's wedding dinner before it spoils, she'll never forgive us."

"Oh, I think she will," Lauren said softly, moaning as his lips brushed lightly across the hollow between her breasts.

"Shall we risk it, then," he asked. Not really waiting for her response, his lips claimed hers, forcing them apart as his tongue probed deeply, dipping into the sweetness of her mouth. Their lips still clinging together, he carried her to the bed, placing her down gently, as though she were a precious, fragile china doll.

The next moment they were a tangle of arms and legs, his hard and muscular, hers soft and silky smooth. Lauren thrilled in the touch of his rough skin as it skimmed across her tender breasts, arousing them to a swollen firmness. Slowly, deliberately, he brought her into the vortex of his passion, lifting her with him. As they moved together in an ultimate moment of surrender and joy, she cried out his name, drawing him tightly into her embrace.

At last, sated and still clasped in each other's arms, they drifted off to sleep. When Lauren awoke, she felt an instant's confusion about where she was.

Two heavy bands of weight across her body only added to her sense of disorientation. Blinking in the room's darkness, she saw Leland lying next to her, one dark arm draped protectively over the paleness of her breasts, his leg thrown across hers.

Suddenly Leland groaned softly and shifted his weight. Lauren was still, hoping he would sleep a few minutes longer so she could study the angles of his face and the long, dark lashes and heavy eyebrows that gave him such a look of fierceness when he was angry. Now, however, the lines of tension that had marred his handsome appearance so often of late were gone, replaced by a look of pure contentment. She smiled to think that she had contributed to that look.

"You seem awfully proud of yourself," he muttered sleepily, catching her expression.

"Do I? All I know is that I've never felt this fulfilled, this much at one with another person before in my life. It's an incredible feeling."

Leland smiled as he ran his hand sensuously along the curves of her body, again igniting her skin with his touch.

"Now you're the one looking smug," she teased as her body reacted to the wondrous sensations he aroused. In turn, she began exploring, searching for his erogenous zones.

Although her expression was determinedly serious, there was a hint of laughter in her eyes as she asked, "What happens if I do this?"

Leland moaned softly, lost for a moment to the sensations she stirred in him.

"And what about this?" she asked innocently, her hands moving across his chest and down his sides.

Suddenly he was laughing and trying frantically to grab her roving hands.

"That tickles, you little minx," he shouted, trying to roll away from her.

"Don't tell me I have found a vulnerability here," she cried, giggling as she pursued him across the bed.

"Get away from me," he insisted, choking with laughter.

"Is that what you really want?" she asked provocatively.

"I'll show you what I really want," he said, capturing her hands at last and pinning her beneath him. She was still chuckling with impish glee when his mouth covered hers, stirring her to breathless excitement once more.

When at long last they looked at the clock, they discovered it was after ten P.M.

"No wonder I'm starving," Leland said. "Bridie's meal is probably ruined by now."

"Maybe not. Why don't I go check while you shower?"

As Lauren had suspected, the housekeeper had obviously anticipated that the newlyweds would not have food on their minds for a while. She had prepared a meal that would not spoil while waiting. An Indonesian chicken dish, with a sauce of honey, garlic, and ginger that improved with time, sat over a low flame in a chafing dish. The salad was still crisp, the dressing in a crystal dish. Fresh strawberries were piled high for dessert, and a bottle of champagne rested on a bed of barely solid ice in a silver cooler. Only the rice, also in a chafing dish, had suffered from the delay. Stirring it lightly with a fork, Lauren saw that even that was not a total loss.

"Well, what do you think?" Leland asked, his arms circling her waist from behind. Lauren could smell the fresh scent of his soap mingling with his own intoxicating masculine scent.

"I don't think we're likely to starve. It appears Bridie expected this," she said with a grin. "Why don't you prove how clever you are by opening the champagne and I'll go take a quick shower of my own."

Before she left she ran her hand along his jaw, roughened with the shadow of a beard. His hair, still damp from his shower, fell into thick waves at her touch. She stood on tiptoes to give him a fleeting kiss.

"Back in a minute."

"No more, or I'll start without you," he warned. "Your stomach may be able to adapt to these little midnight suppers, but mine is distinctly displeased."

When Lauren returned, she was wearing the gown and robe Elsie had given her. She had piled her hair on top of her head in a tangle of loose curls. Leland whistled appreciatively.

"Very nice."

"Thanks. It was a gift from Elsie."

Leland shook his head in wonder. "Henry Cates must be one very lucky man."

"I agree," she said, smiling up at Leland as he seated her at the candlelit table.

A moment later he was lifting his champagne glass in a toast.

"To us," he said, his dark eyes filled with an intensity that startled Lauren.

"To us," she whispered.

As their glasses clinked together, a key rattled in the door of the apartment. Leland's eyes flew in the direction of the noise, his face forming a stonelike mask as the door opened and Gloria Trudeau entered.

Rising, his anger barely under control, Leland started toward her, while Lauren stared after him in a state of shock.

"What are you doing here?" he hissed, his clenched fists and stiff shoulders reflecting his rage.

"Darling," she said breezily, ignoring his attitude and the tension which had filled the room. "I heard you were coming back tonight and I'd hoped to get here first so I could have a wonderful, special meal all ready for you."

Then, as though noticing Lauren for the first time, she added politely, "If I'd known you were bringing someone with you, I would have called first. Is this a client?"

Her casually curious tone did not mask her underlying hostility. Her eyes were cold and carried a warning message as she surveyed the romantic setting and Lauren's attire. Still, she seemed undaunted by her untimely intrusion on an intimate dinner for two. If anything, she seemed to grow more and more self-assured with each passing moment.

When Leland finally spoke, he seemed shaken. "No, Gloria, this is not a client. It's my wife. Lauren, this is Gloria Trudeau."

If the reed-thin blonde was shaken by the announcement, she covered it well. "My goodness, darling, you really should have warned me, asked me to turn in my key or something. I had no idea there was anyone else in your life or I would never have come barging in here tonight."

Her tone was all honeyed sweetness as she turned to Lauren. "Sweetie, I do hope you'll forgive me. I'd hate to see your marriage get off to a bad start because of me."

Lauren had no idea how to handle the hatred she saw in the other woman's eyes. She'd never before encountered someone whose polite phrases bore such a sharp cutting edge. It also seemed to her that Leland was being taken in by the words and not the underlying tone in Gloria's voice. He seemed perfectly willing to believe that this preposterous scene was heading smoothly for a happy ending.

She turned to him with a questioning look, pleading silently with him to throw this intruder out. But Gloria was moving toward him, her intention plain.

To Lauren she said, "I do hope you won't mind if I kiss the groom." She took his face in her hands and looked deeply into his eyes. Her lips, painted a bright red, locked with his and her hands slid through his hair, coming to rest in the still-damp curls at the back of his neck.

In horror Lauren watched as the embrace went on and on in a sort of slow-motion love scene. Choking back her tears, she jumped up from the table, knocking over her chair with a resounding crash that separated Leland and Gloria at last. As Lauren ran from the room, Leland cried out after her, but she was beyond hearing. Instinctively she stumbled into the guest room and locked the door behind her.

Falling onto the bed, her body racked with sobs, she suddenly realized what an impossible contract she'd entered into. She had no doubt that Gloria had some sort of hold on Leland. The mere fact that she had a key to the apartment spoke of an intimacy the woman would not relinquish lightly.

Lost in her own misery, Lauren could not hear the angry exchange of words from the living room. When Leland at last came to the door of the guest room and called out her name, she pretended not to hear him.

"Lauren, please. Can't we talk about this?"

His repeated appeals met with silence and at last he went away, leaving Lauren to spend the remainder of her wedding night feeling more lost and alone than she ever had before.

CHAPTER ELEVEN

When Lauren awoke in the morning, the slate gray of the sky and the steady drizzle of rain outside the apartment reflected her gloomy mood. Hoping that Leland's business meetings had already begun, she crept down the hall to the master bedroom and peeked inside. To her relief it was empty.

Pouring a fragrant bubble bath into the oversized tub, she soaked in the steamy suds, hoping to soothe away some of the questions last night's disastrous ending had raised. After a half-hour, she began to feel the tension ebbing away. Drying herself briskly and splashing on her favorite citrus-scented cologne, she wrapped herself in the thick, royal blue towel and stepped back into the bedroom. Leland was sitting on the bed waiting for her.

"I was just about ready to give up and come in there after you," he said, a tentative smile lifting the corners of his mouth. His eyes raked over her skin, flushed pink by her bath.

"I'm just as glad you didn't," she said stiffly. "Would you mind leaving here while I get dressed?"

"Lauren, for God's sake, we're married. You don't have to hide behind closed doors while you dress," he snapped impatiently.

She stood before him defiantly, clutching the towel tightly around her. When it became clear that she was not about to give in, he walked slowly to the door.

"I'll wait for you in the living room," he informed her flatly. "I'd appreciate it if you could hurry, though. I have a ten o'clock appointment and I'm already running late. I wanted to speak to you before I left."

"Why don't you just go ahead? Nothing you have to say can be that urgent. If it wasn't important enough to bring it up before we got married, then I'm sure it can wait a few more hours," she said, her voice taut with strain.

Leland stood staring at her a moment, frustration and a growing anger etched on his face. He looked ready to explode.

"Fine," he said at last. "If that's the way you want it, we'll talk later. I should be home by five. I hope by then you'll have grown up a bit, so we can discuss this like two adults."

Lauren looked as though he'd slapped her, and for an instant it appeared he would apologize. Instead he took a handful of bills from his wallet and tossed them at her.

"Meantime, go shopping or something. Bridie can

direct you to Saks or Bloomingdale's. Or you can go to F.A.O. Schwarz and buy a toy to take back to Holly."

He left then, slamming the door behind him. Tears streamed down Lauren's face as she stared after him. Finally she forced herself to splash some cold water on her puffy, reddened eyes. Carefully applied makeup disguised most of the damage wrought by the morning's crying and a bright yellow blouse edged in navy blue, worn with her new navy suit, perked up her spirits, so she felt able to face Bridie.

If the housekeeper was aware of the strain between Lauren and Leland, she kept her knowledge to herself. When Lauren went into the kitchen in search of some coffee, Bridie greeted her cheerfully, insisted that she have some freshly baked coffee cake with her coffee, and then sat down opposite her at the kitchen table.

"I hope you don't think it presumptuous of me sitting down and joining you like this," she said.

"No, of course not. I'm glad of the company," Lauren admitted truthfully.

"You could've knocked my Jim and me over with a feather when we heard the news from Mr. Cross," Bridie offered confidentially. "But, lass, I can see right off that you'll be good for him. You're not like . . . well, like some others I could name. If I can give you a wee bit of advice—you just be patient with him. He's been a bachelor for a mighty long time and changing his ways won't come easy for him. He's stubborn as a mule, but don't let that bother you. You just stand right up to him. The man loves you. Anybody can see that. You give him a little time and he'll be the best husband any woman could hope for."

Hesitantly, Lauren looked up at Bridie, her eyes revealing her pain and doubt. "You really think he loves me?" she asked, trying to hide her feeling of desperation.

"Why, of course, he loves you," Bridie insisted, sounding shocked that Lauren could doubt it. "He married you, didn't he? Let me tell you something, little Laurie. There've been plenty of women in Mr. Cross's life. They've paraded through here so fast sometimes, it's made my head swim. But there's not a one of 'em he's ever asked to marry him, not a one who's even been around more than a few weeks. You take my word for it, he loves you or you wouldn't be Mrs. Leland Cross."

A tiny spark of hope ignited in Lauren's heart, and as the morning wore on, she was able to fan it into a full-fledged fire. She was able to convince herself that everything Bridie had told her made perfect sense, that Leland must love her even if he was not yet ready to admit it, even to himself. Deterred by the rain, she decided to spend the rest of the day at the apartment, trying to sort out her feelings and prepare for her encounter with Leland in the evening.

Shortly after noon Bridie left to do the marketing and Lauren settled herself on the floor in the living room, where she'd found an old family album she hoped would give her some hints about Leland's past. Sipping a cup of coffee, a jazz album on the stereo in the background, she was just beginning to relax when the doorbell rang.

There, looking sleek and sophisticated despite the weather, stood Gloria Trudeau, her lips drawn back in a mockery of a smile. Lauren's eyes widened at the sight of her.

"You," Lauren said, her shock registering in her voice.

"Surprised to see me," the woman asked sweetly. "You shouldn't be, you know."

She brushed past Lauren without waiting for an invitation to enter. Throwing her rain-soaked coat carelessly over the back of a chair, she settled down on the sofa, took a cigarette from a gold case, and lit it. She watched the rising puffs of smoke as though fascinated by them. When at last she turned back to Lauren, her look was filled with disdain.

"I really can't imagine what you and I have to discuss," Lauren said haltingly, furious that she was unable to match the other woman's poise.

"Really? Of course it's evident that you and I have very little in common," Gloria said, her voice dripping with sarcasm. "However, there is Lee."

"Who happens to be my husband," Lauren interjected forcefully.

"For how long? You can't honestly expect to hold on to a man like Leland Cross. Oh, I'm sure he finds you fascinating enough for the moment. You're certainly not like his usual women. You have a certain naive charm that's very appealing to a man like Lee. It makes him feel protective. But I assure you he'll tire of the role."

"I don't think so, Ms. Trudeau. Lee loves me," she asserted defiantly, her look daring contradiction. Gloria merely laughed at her, though the laughter

133

never reached her eyes, which were cold and calculating.

"Oh, darling, you are such a babe-in-the-woods, aren't you? Don't you know that love is a myth? When it comes right down to it, all that romantic nonsense won't hold a man. I know Lee. He may think he wants a cozy little house with a doting wife making pot roast every Sunday, but pretty soon all that will bore him to tears."

The biting remarks were eating away at Lauren's self-confidence. Secretly she had to admit that Gloria was voicing some of her own doubts about how long Leland would be satisfied with an old-fashioned, settled homelife. This was his world, this Manhattan apartment with its decorator touches, its modern art, and its spectacular view. He belonged with people like Gloria Trudeau—beautiful people who led challenging, exciting lives. His was a world of travel, of constant intellectual stimulation, of art galleries and museums, of ballets and concerts, of gourmet restaurants and late-night suppers.

With all of that, Lauren wondered how soon Leland would tire of Charleston's eighteenth-century charm, its slow pace, and her own family-oriented values. She rarely made pot roast, as Gloria had scathingly suggested, but she did not make beef Wellington either. Her culinary achievements, like her life-style, ran toward the plain and simple.

There was a gleam of satisfaction in Gloria's eyes as she watched the effect her words were having on Lauren. She pushed her advantage.

"I want you to remember one more thing. I will use anything to get Lee back and, frankly, once I start going after him, I don't think it will take very long."

Her warning given, she picked up her coat and left, leaving a stunned and shaken Lauren staring after her. Lauren had no doubt the woman meant exactly what she said. Certainly Lee had found her attractive once. How long would it be before he gave in to her seductive pull again? No man, not even a saint, could ignore the impact of an alluring body offered willingly and without strings. And innocent though she might be, Lauren knew that was exactly what Gloria intended to offer.

Distraught, she left the apartment to wander blindly in the direction of Central Park. She was oblivious to the storm, which was picking up and drenching her uncovered hair and causing her to shiver inside her thin coat. She felt an actual physical pain at the thought of losing Leland so soon after finding him, but perhaps it was better to give him up now rather than fight for him for months only to lose him in the end anyway. At last she made up her mind. She would go back to Charleston, let Leland out of their farce of a marriage, and resume her own lonely, sterile existence with Holly.

Back at the apartment, she interrupted Bridie's clucking disapproval of her walking about in the rain.

"Bridie, please, I'll be just fine. I'm only a little wet."

"Soaked through is more like it."

"Bridie, is Jim around?"

"Not right this minute. He took Mr. Cross to an

appointment, but he should be back here in a half-hour or so. Why?" she asked.

"Do you suppose he could take me to La-Guardia?" Lauren asked. "Or should I just take a cab?"

"LaGuardia?" Bridie repeated. "Why on earth would you be wanting to go to the airport, miss?"

"Please. No questions, Bridie. I just have to get back to Charleston."

"Does Mr. Cross know you're leaving?"

"No," Lauren nearly shouted. "And he's not to be told either. I'll . . . I'll leave him a note explaining."

"Don't you want me to call him, Miss Laurie? He'll be fit to be tied if he comes home and finds you've just packed your bags and gone off without a word."

"I'm sorry, Bridie. It has to be this way. Now can Jim take me or not?"

"Of course he'll take you, child," she said soothingly, her expression a mixture of concern and dismay.

Jim, though reluctant to comply with Lauren's request, went along with it once Bridie convinced him of her determination to leave no matter how she had to get to the airport. At LaGuardia he gave her an awkward embrace before watching her go off dejectedly toward the ticket counter.

Lauren had barely enough time to buy her ticket and run to the gate. On board, there was a brief moment before takeoff when she had second thoughts, but then the plane was in the air and it was too late to turn back. As the jet climbed into the darkening sky she looked down and thought of all she was leaving behind. Her tears, unshed until now, spilled over and rolled down her cheeks.

It was late in the evening by the time she reached her house. She decided not to tell Sue of her return. She could use a night alone to think things through and determine what her next move should be. A part of her wanted to take Holly and run away, escaping from all of the questions which were bound to come once people heard what had happened. Deep down, though, she knew that would be foolish. Financially she needed the security of her job in Reed's office. And once Leland's bargain with the city was struck and finalized, perhaps there would be no more uncomfortable encounters with him to endure. She could pick up the pieces of her life.

In the morning, once Holly had left for school, she went next door to see Sue.

"Lauren! What are you doing back already? I didn't expect you for days." Sue's ever-bubbling well of enthusiasm dried up when she saw her friend's despondency.

"Honey, what is it?"

At the sympathetic tone Lauren burst into tears and allowed Sue to lead her into the house, settle her into a chair, and bring her tissues and some hot tea. Finally she grew calm.

"Now then, can you talk about it?"

Faltering, Lauren tried to explain what had happened—Gloria's intrusion on her wedding night, her follow-up visit, and threats.

"So I decided to leave. It was all wrong from the beginning. I should have recognized that it couldn't work. People like me do not marry people like Leland Cross," she concluded with a weary sigh.

"What do you mean, people like you?" Sue asked indignantly. "You're one of the finest people I've ever known. You're good and kind. You're bright. You've got a great future ahead of you as an architect. You're a terrific mother. Holly adores you and she's growing up in a home filled with love and support. Why isn't that good enough for Leland Cross?"

"It's just not. I might as well admit it. It was all a dream, a lovely dream that couldn't survive the realistic, harsh light of day."

Sue recognized that there was no reasoning with Lauren in her present state. "So what will you do?" she asked.

"I'll divorce him, go back to work, and pretty soon it'll be as though the whole thing never happened."

Lauren stayed with Sue throughout the morning and was waiting there when Holly came home from school.

"Mommy," she squealed in delight. "You're home! I missed you."

"I missed you too, pumpkin," Lauren said, holding her tightly as she blinked back a fresh batch of tears.

"Where's Lee? Is he home too," she asked, dancing about excitedly.

Lauren tried to keep her voice steady. "No, honey. Lee's still in New York. I'm sure he'll be back in a few days."

"When he comes back will he be my new daddy and live with us?"

Lauren shook her head miserably. Holly's eyes showed her disbelief. "But, Mommy, you promised. You said we'd be a family, just like before . . ." Her tiny voice broke off and she ran crying to the comfort of Sue's arms. Helplessly Lauren stood bereft, understanding Holly's feeling of betrayal.

"Baby, you and me, we're a family," she offered.

"Not a real one with a mommy and a daddy," Holly insisted, clinging tightly to Sue as she regarded her mother with accusing eyes.

"Holly, I know you don't understand this," Sue interjected, "but what your mother says is true. You are a real family. You're two people who love each other and take care of each other. That's all a family really is."

Holly's lower lip trembled and tears slid down her cheeks. "But I wanted a daddy so bad."

"I know you did, pumpkin, and I'm sorry it didn't work out. But Lee does love you, you know. You can still be friends," Lauren said, holding out her arms as Holly ran to her.

Later that night Lauren sat propped up in bed, unable to sleep. Holly, who had begged to stay with her just this once, was curled up asleep at her side. Lauren reached out and brushed the damp curls from her flushed cheeks.

"Baby, I just hope I can keep this promise," she whispered softly. "I pray Lee won't hate me so much for running out on him that he'll take it out on you."

Deep in her heart, she was sure he wouldn't.

CHAPTER TWELVE

Although Lauren knew she could stay away from the office for a few more days, she decided she might as well go in immediately and get things over with. The sooner she faced Elsie and Reed the better. Besides, she needed to get on with her life and start filling the hours. Too much time alone to think about Leland and Gloria would be fatal.

As soon as she walked through the office door, Elsie jumped up to give her a hug.

"Welcome home, Lauren. I wondered if you'd be in today."

Lauren studied her closely, surprised at her nonchalance.

"You know, don't you?" she asked, her voice cracking slightly.

When Elsie nodded, giving her hand a squeeze, Lauren asked, "How?"

"It doesn't matter."

141

"Yes, it does," Lauren insisted. "Lee called you, didn't he?"

"Yes," Elsie admitted finally. "He didn't say too much, though, just that there'd been a misunderstanding and you had come home alone."

Lauren was shaking her head. "It was no misunderstanding, Elsie. The marriage was a mistake. That's all."

"I don't believe that. Lauren, I don't know what happened between the two of you, but that man is miserable. He loves you and you walked out on him."

"Is that what he told you?" Lauren asked skeptically.

"No. I told you that Lee didn't say much. But, honey, it doesn't take a genius to tell that he's hurting. Frankly, you don't look any too happy yourself."

"Of course I'm not happy," Lauren snapped. "But this is the best thing for both of us. You'll just have to take my word for it, Elsie."

"Well, I'm sorry, but I can't do that. I want you two to sit down and work out your differences. Will you promise me you'll try to do that," she pleaded.

"Oh, Elsie, I love you for caring so much, but it's no use. It's been over twenty-four hours since I left and Lee hasn't even called. That hardly sounds like a man who wants desperately to work things out."

"Did you honestly expect him to drop everything and follow you? Is that what you hoped to accomplish by running away?" Elsie asked heatedly. "Lauren Cross, I'm ashamed of you. I thought you were too mature to play games with someone you loved."

"I wasn't playing games. I had to leave. Elsie, you just don't know what it was like. That . . . that woman coming in there on our wedding night, acting as though she owned the place. Then she came back again the next day to warn me that she wouldn't stop until she had Lee back again."

"So you just gave up without a fight? You let her win?"

"She was right. Lee needs someone like her, someone glamorous and exciting." Lauren's tears, never far from the surface, started to brim over. Elsie held her tightly and patted her back.

"There, there. You go on and cry," she said soothingly. When Lauren's sobs had subsided, Elsie sat back and looked at her. "You know something, my dear, if I didn't love you like a daughter, I'd be inclined to think you were a little dull-witted."

"What . . ." Lauren sputtered, her voice trailing off.

"If Lee had wanted that woman, whoever she is, don't you think he'd have married her? I've never known Leland Cross not to go after exactly whatever or whomever he wanted. If I were you, I'd stop and think a good, long time about that before I went and threw him back to that lioness."

For the rest of the morning, Lauren had little time to think. Elsie and Reed seemed to have conspired to see that she was so busy she wouldn't have time to become depressed. There were reports to type, files to update, and at ten A.M. a meeting with the mayor which Reed insisted she attend so he would have a

143

record of the conversation, some of which dealt with Leland's project. It was apparent the mayor wanted to find some way to salvage the proposal, despite mounting opposition from the preservationists.

"I can understand their side of it," the mayor admitted with a heavy sigh. "That's what makes this so difficult. We want to keep historic buildings whenever possible. We want to maintain the integrity of our architectural style. But, damn it all, at some point we have to give in a little if we expect Charleston to move into the twentieth century."

"I agree with you," Reed said. "But is this the right project on which to pin that move?"

"I thought you were behind the Cross tower," the mayor said, his tone surprised.

"I am. As far as I'm concerned, there will never be a better one. Lee knows exactly what he's doing."

"Well, then, I think we bite the bullet on this one and take the flak from the public."

"Do you think the councilmen will go along with you?" Reed asked skeptically.

"Well, that newspaper story didn't help, but, yes, I think we've got the votes to push it through. Cross will be back in plenty of time for that meeting, won't he?"

"Absolutely. I talked with him again this morning. He said he'd be back by tomorrow at the latest. We'll have a couple of weeks to sit down and hammer out all the details before the November first hearing."

Lauren tried not to show her surprise at Reed's announcement. She realized the irony in it. Her boss knew more about her husband's schedule than she did.

She thought about that and about what Elsie had told her earlier as she walked through the shops and galleries of the public market during her lunch hour. Because of all the little craft and antique stores, it was one of her favorite places for shopping for gifts. Holly loved it because of the ice cream parlors.

She crossed a street into a cavernous open building which housed fruit and vegetable stalls and picked up some fresh produce to take home, including a pumpkin for Holly to carve for Halloween. She'd already gotten her a Wonder Woman costume.

The shopping distracted Lauren for a while, but eventually her thoughts returned to Leland and their impetuous marriage. Marry in haste, repent at leisure. How many times had she heard that old cliché back when she and Doug had rushed into marriage while still in college? But their relationship, for all that it had lacked in excitement, had had a certain stability based on a mutual respect and need. With Lee she had the reverse—excitement, but nothing enduring.

For a brief moment she wondered if Elsie could possibly be right, that Lee did love her and she had made a tragic mistake by abandoning him. Then she thought of Gloria, and her doubts were dispelled. She could not compete with her beauty, her cleverness, and most of all her determination to have Leland back.

It was after two by the time she got back to the office and the remainder of the afternoon sped by. As five o'clock neared, she began to dread the thought of going home. Apparently Elsie sensed her feelings.

"Why don't you go pick up Holly and come to dinner with Henry and me," she suggested.

When Lauren appeared ready to decline, she added, "I've got some wonderful fresh mackerel. Henry went fishing today. If you all don't come, I'll have fish smelling up the house for days."

Laughing, Lauren agreed. "Okay. We'd love to. How soon would you like us?"

"You just get Holly and come right on over."

An hour later Henry was welcoming them, his normally taciturn demeanor warming as always to Holly's exuberance. While Lauren went to help Elsie in the kitchen, he took Holly up to the attic and saw her settled playing dress-up with the old taffeta and lace gowns and flower-trimmed hats that filled half a dozen dusty trunks.

Downstairs he joined the women in the large country kitchen. Pipe in hand, he was content to sit back and listen to their chatter, offering only an occasional pithy comment that made them both laugh. Henry's terseness was a perfect counterpoint to Elsie's loquacity and Lauren had come to love him for his wisdom and his warm heart.

At dinner everyone was lavish in their praise of Henry's catch and Elsie's delicious preparation of the mackerel and acorn squash, which she'd baked with butter and cinnamon. For dessert there was pecan pie with homemade ice cream.

"Elsie, if you keep cooking like this, Henry's going to wind up weighing three hundred pounds," Lauren teased.

"Not old skin 'n' bones," Elsie said, eying her husband's lanky six-foot frame, which didn't have an ounce of excess flab anywhere. "I'm the one who's going to gain it all. I swear I pick up an extra pound of water just by going outside and breathing on a humid day."

"You look just fine to me," Henry offered, giving her a friendly pinch as she passed by on her way to the kitchen.

When the dishes had been cleared away, they all went into the old-fashioned parlor with its lace curtains and crocheted doilies on all the tabletops. The flowered wallpaper and white woodwork all spoke of another era. Henry sat down at the piano after a little encouragement from Holly, and they all sang. The time passed so pleasantly that Lauren was surprised to hear the grandfather clock chime ten.

"I'd better get my little one here on home. She's got school in the morning."

Holly started to protest, but a giant yawn overtook her and she sleepily gave in.

"Elsie, Henry, thank you both," Lauren said, hugging them both gratefully.

"Will you be okay?" Elsie asked with concern.

"Of course. Don't worry about me. I've caused you too many problems already."

"Nonsense. You need us, you call. You and Holly are welcome here any time," Henry said, putting Holly down in the front seat of the car and closing the door.

Lauren thought about the couple's kindness on the drive home. How different her life might have been had her own parents had a similar knack for caring. Instead, they had always made her feel that her presence was a burden, her problems unimportant. She hoped that no matter how harried her own life became, she would never dismiss Holly that easily, would never make her feel unwanted and unloved.

At home she carried the now sleeping child to the front door. As she stood on the porch trying to shift Holly in her arms so she could fit the key into the lock, the door opened. Silently Leland reached out and took Holly from her. Startled and dismayed to find him inside her house, Lauren stood there, unable to resist or even to speak. Finally she followed him inside. By the time he returned from putting Holly to bed, she had herself under control.

"How did you get in here?" she demanded, facing him defiantly.

"I hardly think that's important."

"I think it is. Breaking and entering is against the law, even for Leland Cross!"

He smiled lazily, settling back comfortably in the easy chair. He was clearly unaffected by her mounting anger.

"You don't really think I'd stoop to breaking in, do you?" he asked curiously. "Come to think of it, I'm not at all sure it's possible for a man to break into his own home."

"Your home?" she shouted. "This is my home!"

"No, my dear, it's ours, now that we're married. Or have you forgotten that little technicality?"

"Why, you . . . you . . ."

"You what? Scoundrel? Liar? Cheat?"

She looked at him in confusion.

"Surely you don't intend to . . . to live here," she said, her voice filled with disbelief.

"Oh, but I do. You and I married for better or

148

worse, and I told you then that I did not take those words lightly. So, it's up to you, Lauren. Will it be for better or for worse? You decide."

"I can't," she whispered at last. "I need time."

Her face pale, her eyes troubled, she appealed to him. "Please, Lee, couldn't you stay on at your own place for a while?"

"No!" His tone was final. "We live together. Now we can do that in marital bliss or in an armed truce, but there is no other alternative."

"But this house, it's not big enough. It only has two . . ." Her voice faltered.

"Two bedrooms? We don't need any more than that. Holly has hers and you and I have ours."

"You can't be serious."

"Lauren, for the last time, I am deadly serious."

Lauren recognized the look of determination on his face and knew it was futile to argue any longer. Her head was throbbing anyway, and she couldn't think clearly.

"I'm tired, Lee. Can't we talk about this some more in the morning?"

"We can talk about it all you like, whenever you like, but our basic situation won't change. We're married and we're staying that way," he said forcefully, his eyes boring into her. Finally he sighed and turned away. "You go on to bed. I'll be in later."

Lauren flew from the room, her whirling thoughts increasing the pounding in her head. A couple of aspirin and a hot shower helped some, but in bed her feeling of panic returned as she waited for Leland to join her. She lay there stiffly, her hands clenching the sheets, her eyes wide with alarm at each sound that might signal his approach. But when eventually she drifted off, he still had not come.

In the morning a pillow and rumpled blanket on the sofa explained why. Her eyes were questioning when she joined him and an excited Holly in the kitchen for breakfast.

"Mommy, I thought you said Lee wasn't going to come live with us."

"Apparently I made a mistake," she said, ignoring his smug look of satisfaction.

Although Holly was oblivious to the tension in the air, Lauren's nerves were taut from the strain of making polite conversation. When she could stand it no longer, she announced it was time to take Holly to school.

"We can drop her off on our way to City Hall," Leland agreed smoothly.

"But—" Lauren began. Leland promptly interrupted.

"There's no need for us to take two cars. I can always come back for you at five if I happen to be away later in the day. But I suspect with this hearing coming up, I'll be spending most of my time at City Hall these days anyway."

Lauren shrugged in a gesture of defeat. It was useless to fight over something so trivial, not when there were so many major unresolved issues facing them.

The rest of the day began to set the pattern for all the days to come. Leland continued to sleep on the sofa. Breakfasts were strained but bearable. During the day Leland was busy with meetings and they rarely spent a moment alone. He was frequently tied up with conferences late into the night as the November date for the public hearing on the tower neared. They shared an uncomfortable coexistence, but little more. Leland seemed reluctant to pursue their original argument and Lauren so dreaded a repetition of it that she was grateful for the reprieve.

She forced herself to continue taking the urban planning class on Thursday nights, finding that only there was she able to put aside her personal involvement with Leland and see him merely as a respected expert in his field. This time she would allow nothing to deter her from going on to get her degree.

Besides, she enjoyed the interaction with the other students, none of whom knew about her marriage. Rod, particularly, was becoming a good friend. Although he didn't quite understand her refusal to join the group for coffee after class, he accepted it. Occasionally he called her at the office to check up on her or to talk about the next week's assignment. One Friday, after she'd seemed particularly blue in class the previous night, he called and invited her to lunch.

Lauren hesitated.

"Come on. It'll do you good. I'm sure Reed Donovan keeps things so hectic over there that you can use a break," he argued persuasively.

"You're right. A break will do me good." She could see no real harm in an innocuous lunch with a friend.

They met at a seafood restaurant which was relatively inexpensive despite its fine reputation for lobster dainties and fish stuffed with crabmeat. Rod was right. The pleasant atmosphere, the excellent food, and the friendly, casual conversation were just what she needed. She felt more relaxed than she had since the entire nightmare with Leland had begun.

They were sipping a second cup of coffee when Rod broached the subject of her recent behavior. Taking her hand gently in his, he asked, "All right, kid, tell Uncle Rod. What's been bothering you lately?"

"Nothing." She lied unconvincingly. "I'm just a little tired and run down."

He shook his head. "No good, Lauren. It's more than that. You look as though, I don't know, as though you'd been betrayed, badly hurt by someone you care about. Please, can't you talk about it? Maybe I can help."

Lauren gave his hand a squeeze.

"You know, you're very special, Rod Stevens. I don't know what I'd do without you," she said softly, looking at him warmly.

Suddenly a shadow fell over their table and Lauren looked up to see Leland looming over them, his face taut with anger.

"I hope I'm not interrupting anything," he apologized sarcastically.

"No, of course not, Mr. Cross," Rod said, puzzled by his instructor's obvious wrath. "Would you like to join us?"

Leland's eyes never wavered from Lauren's face, which was flushed with embarrassment.

"No, I don't think so," he said finally. "I'm with some business associates and I must get back to them. I just wanted to stop by and say hello."

To Lauren he added pointedly, "You and I will talk later."

Nodding curtly to Rod, he moved through the crowded restaurant toward his own table. Lauren could see from the way he carried himself that his rage was barely under control. She dreaded the moment when she had to deal with the accusations that were bound to come. But first she would have to face Rod and his questions. Reluctantly she raised her eyes to his.

"I'm sorry you had to become involved in all of this," she said, her chin quivering as tears threatened to roll down her cheeks.

"Involved in all of what?" Rod asked in confusion. "Lauren, what does Leland Cross have to do with you and whatever's troubling you?"

"He's . . . he's my husband," she whispered, her voice breaking.

"Your what?" Rod's astonishment at her announcement could not have been any more complete had she told him the man was a vampire and she his latest target.

"It's a long story."

"We've got plenty of time," he said soothingly. "Tell me about it. You weren't married when the class started, were you?"

"No. We've just been married a couple of weeks."

"But I didn't even think you knew him. You even said he asked if you were the Lauren Mitchell working for the planning director."

"I just said that so no one would think we were friends. I didn't think it would matter. We really did barely know each other," she said, her voice pleading for his understanding.

"How did you wind up getting married that quickly?"

"It just happened. Leland can be very persuasive when he wants something badly enough. You've seen him in action trying to get this office tower approved by the city council. What chance did I have against him?"

Rod glanced across the restaurant at the darkly handsome man, who was gazing at them fiercely.

"I see what you mean. So you married him. And now things aren't going too smoothly?"

"Smoothly," Lauren said bitterly. "It's a disaster. I never should have allowed him to talk me into it. But I . . . I loved him. I thought I could make it work in time."

Rod studied her closely, sharing her pain. Gently he asked, "And now you don't think it can?"

She shook her head miserably. "There's someone else. She's rich and gorgeous and she wants him back. I'm sure if he'd taken the time to stop and think about it, he would have realized that Gloria Trudeau is the woman he really loves. They come from the same world—a world where the air's so rarefied mere mortals like you and me can't survive in it."

A few minutes later they finished their coffee and left. Lauren tried not to look at Leland as she passed near his table and Rod put a comforting arm across her shoulders, whispering a bit of nonsense in her ear to make her smile as they exited.

That night Lauren sat up until nearly midnight, waiting for Leland to come home. She wanted to get their confrontation over with. Finally her apprehensiveness gave way to exhaustion, and she fell asleep on the sofa, tossing and turning restlessly as an angry Leland floated in and out of her dreams.

When she awoke shortly after dawn, she realized he had not come home at all. She was torn between worry that something had happened to him and fury at his lack of consideration in not calling. Despite the strains in their marriage, they had maintained the polite amenities. Never before had he failed to notify her if he was planning to be late. Now even that simple courtesy appeared to have been scrapped. It seemed the last blow the shaky foundation of their marriage could take.

Lauren went through the motions of normalcy, getting Holly ready for school and herself ready for work. But her heart wasn't in it. She kept seeing the look of outrage on Leland's face when he'd come over to speak to her and Rod. Why had he been so furious, she wondered. Surely he wasn't jealous. The thought was almost ludicrous. Rod was so much younger than she was. Besides, they were only friends. He'd never even made a mild pass at her.

Still she couldn't shake the memory of that look on Leland's face. It was still puzzling her at mid-morning when she looked up to find Gloria walking breezily through the door of her office. This was the final straw.

"What do you want?" she snapped.

"My, my, aren't we cheerful this morning? Have a bad night, Lauren?" she inquired sweetly.

Lauren stared at her coldly. "I asked you what you wanted."

"I just came by to thank you."

"Thank me? For what?"

"For giving up so quickly. It's much more painless this way for everyone. I know Lee is grateful," she said, her eyes glinting with delight at Lauren's confusion and discomfort.

"You've seen Lee?" Lauren questioned, her voice faltering.

"Of course, darling. He was with me last night."

Her words were like a knife twisting in Lauren's abdomen. "He was with you?"

"You didn't know?" Gloria asked, her surprise echoing falsely. "Oh, my. I just assumed he had told you. Well, never mind. I'm sure he'll tell you all about it when he's ready. You know how unimportant little details tend to slip by busy men."

Her mission accomplished, Gloria turned quickly to leave. In her hurry she bumped right into Leland, who had a ten thirty appointment with Reed.

For a moment her composure slipped ever so slightly, but she quickly recovered. Kissing him on the cheek, she said, "Darling! Good morning. I've just been visiting with Lauren."

"Why?" he asked quietly.

"Oh, just a little girl talk. Now I've got to run. I'll see you later, sweetheart," she said briskly and was gone.

"What was that all about?" Leland asked, turning to Lauren.

"Nothing," she said abruptly. "Mr. Donovan's waiting for you. You can go right in."

"Lauren, we need to talk."

"I don't think there's anything else to talk about," she said wearily. Then, determination in her voice, she told him, "I want a divorce. If you want grounds, I think adultery will do. Now, if you don't mind, I have work to do."

She picked up a stack of letters which needed to be mailed and walked out, praying that he would not notice her trembling. Stunned, he stood there staring after her.

CHAPTER THIRTEEN

As soon as the office door had closed behind her, Lauren leaned against the wall for support. Her knees were buckling and she suddenly felt faint. She was still standing in the same spot when a secretary from a neighboring office stepped out into the hall.

Rushing to Lauren's side, she asked, "Lauren, are you okay? You look about ready to keel over."

"I'm just a little shaky, Peg. I'm sure I'll be fine in a minute."

"Here," Peg said, offering her arm, "Let me help you to the ladies room."

In the lounge the old leather sofa felt marvelously cool against Lauren's feverish skin. Leaning back with a damp towel over her eyes, she began to feel better. The trembling stopped and the faintness passed.

"You're looking a little better now," Peg said, "but you probably ought to stay here a little longer.

Give me those letters and I'll take them along to the post office when I go."

"Thanks, Peg. You're an angel."

"Hardly," she quipped with a wink. "Now if you don't feel absolutely perfect in a few minutes you tell Mr Donovan and take the rest of the day off."

"I will," Lauren agreed, knowing that it wouldn't be necessary. Her "illness" was only temporary, a bad case of too much Gloria Trudeau and Leland Cross. She'd recover in due time.

Recalling the look of shock on Leland's face when she'd flung her demand for a divorce at him, she had a moment's regret. What if Elsie was right and she was just playing into Gloria's hands?

No, she told herself sharply. *It's done now and I know it's the right thing to do. It has to be.*

She just prayed he wouldn't fight her. She knew her emotions could not hold out for long against Leland's powerful influence because, despite everything that had happened, she still loved him desperately.

Back in her office, the sight of Reed's closed door indicated he was still meeting with Leland. The thought of another encounter made Lauren's trembling start all over again. She buzzed Reed on the intercom and apologized for interrupting.

"Would you mind terribly if I took an early lunch break," she asked, a quiet desperation so evident in her voice that he agreed immediately.

"No problem. Take as long as you like. Go for a walk. If I have to leave before you get back, I'll have the switchboard pick up our calls."

Lauren decided to take his advice and walk. Exercise was the best antidepressant she could think of, especially on this clear, crisp October morning. The sky was a brilliant blue scattered with powder puffs of white. The air was pungent with the scent of burning leaves.

As she strolled along, she wondered why fall had always been her favorite season when spring was supposed to be symbolic of new beginnings. And Charleston's springs, she had to admit, were something to behold. Nearly every yard was a veritable painter's palette of shades of green splashed with the vibrant pink, deep purple, and pure white of the azaleas. Sometimes she wished she could paint, perhaps in the Impressionistic style of Monet, so she could capture those colors.

But spring seemed to her too gentle, with its soft breezes and light showers, with its tiny new plants thrusting up through the earth, struggling to live. Fall had none of that tentativeness, that uncertainty about it. It was like a man in mid-life, who has the boldness that comes from knowledge and self-awareness, who is yet unafraid of the future and its inevitable end. Fall's winds are full-bodied, and today, chilling her skin through the thin silk of her blouse, they made Lauren feel alive.

Her spirits lifted even higher as the bells of St. Michael's rang out behind her. Their joyous sound, so much a part of the city's history, made her smile for a fleeting moment.

Continuing her aimless walk, she wandered through the wrought iron gateway into Washington Park, a patch of midtown greenery rife with testaments to Charleston's past. It seemed to Lauren that the statues of British statesman William Pitt and of Henry Timrod, poet laureate of the confederacy, said a great deal about the city's love for both its history and its culture. Most of the people she knew would be far more comfortable sitting around talking about art and music than they would be downing martinis in a raucous disco.

Finally, drawn to the peace and serenity of the churchyard at St. Philip's, Lauren strolled among the tombstones, touched by the sentimental epitaphs she read. There was something infinitely calming about this place, where the great such as John C. Calhoun were resting eternally alongside families known and loved only by their own. Dates on some of the markers were a poignant reminder of how many children were wiped out by diseases that are no longer a threat even to children Holly's age.

As Lauren left the churchyard, she realized how close she was to the Dock Street Theater and walked over to it. Checking the posters for the current production, she made a mental note to herself to see if Sue would like to go one night. They hadn't been to the theater since last winter. Lauren had even missed the productions during the Spoleto Festival in the spring because of Doug's illness. Even though he'd urged her to go, she had been unwilling to leave his side except to eat and sleep.

By the time she returned to the office, Leland had left. There was no note on her desk. Nor did he call during the afternoon. At home that night she discovered why there had been no word from him. He had moved out. That was his response to her demand for a divorce. All his clothes had been removed from the bedroom closet and a note propped on the dresser offered nothing more than a phone number where he could be reached. Lauren crumpled the note, her body wracked with sobs. Although this was what she had claimed to want, she was devastated by the reality of it.

"Mommy, what's wrong?" Holly asked hesitantly from the doorway. Her own lips were quivering at the sight of Lauren's distress and panic filled her eyes.

Unable to speak, Lauren gathered the child into her arms and held her tightly, rocking her back and forth. Holly clung to her and pleaded, "Please, Mommy. Tell me. I'm scared."

"Oh, baby, no. Don't be scared. Everything's all right. Mommy just had some bad news."

"Not like when Daddy died?"

"No. Of course not. Nothing like that," she said reassuringly. "It's just that Lee . . . Lee has gone away. He won't be living here anymore."

"But why, Mommy? I love Lee."

"I know you do. But this is the way it has to be. I know you don't understand now, but someday maybe you will. Maybe we both will."

The next morning, after a sleepless night, Lauren picked up the paper and saw the headline announcing the day's public hearing on Leland's project. Again Mason Hart had written the story, indicating that the preservationists and other opponents were ready to do battle in the council chambers. There were comments from the mayor pleading for the city's residents to be rational in their approach to the plans for the tower. And there was an unflattering picture of Leland that made him appear just as cold and calculating as the opposition believed him to be.

The story threw Lauren for just a moment. Somehow she had forgotten that today was the scheduled hearing date. It meant she would have to see Leland, would have to spend most of the day with him, first in Reed's office and then later upstairs in the council chambers. For a fleeting moment she thought of calling Elsie and asking her to fill in, but she dismissed the idea as cowardly. Sooner or later she and Leland would have to meet anyway. It might as well be today.

Outside City Hall there were already signs of the impending fight. Picketers bearing placards saying, YANKEE GO HOME; PARKS, NOT OFFICES and SAVE OUR LANDMARKS were some of the more polite opponents. Once inside, Lauren watched from her window as the crowd grew in size. When Leland's car pulled into a space nearby and he began walking to the building, a few of those marching recognized him. As word of his approach spread, jeers and catcalls went up, taunting him. Lauren admired the way he reacted. He spoke to those he knew, ignoring the confusion around him. His pace remained casual and unhurried, as though none of this was directed at him.

When he reached the planning director's office, his composure had slipped ever so slightly. Lauren could see the pain in his eyes as he looked at her, and her heart tumbled erratically.

"Reed's waiting for you," she managed at last, trying to tear her eyes away from his.

At first it seemed he was about to speak, but finally

he simply nodded and walked past her. She followed him in.

"Can I get you both some coffee? It looks as though it's going to be a very long day," she said.

"Don't let the women's libbers hear you offering to get coffee, Lauren. They'll tar and feather you," Reed said, trying to lighten the atmosphere.

Lauren poured two cups from the electric coffee-pot at the back of the office and handed them to the men.

"That's always seemed to me to be one of their sillier battles," she observed. "I see no reason why I shouldn't get your coffee for you when you're busy. Seems to me that's simply consideration, not sexism."

"See what a jewel I have here," Reed said proudly to Leland. Then, flustered by the remark, he coughed nervously and added, "I mean . . . of course, you know."

There was an awkward pause before he went on. "Now then," he said at last, "let's see what we need to do before the meeting begins."

As Leland and Reed compared notes, Lauren watched the man who would soon be her ex-husband. It was as though she wanted to absorb every detail about him, the broad shoulders and rippling muscles of his chest, covered now with an impeccable three-piece gray suit and a pinstriped shirt, all just conservative enough to impress Charleston's residents with his sincerity. Lauren studied his face, noting the slight frown that wrinkled his brow, the sensual lips, the tiny crinkles at the corners of his eyes, testimony to the laughter of happier times.

165

Suddenly he looked up from his diagrams and his eyes met hers. There was a question in them, a question and a longing that shook Lauren to her very core. Then they turned the cold gray of steel and he looked away, leaving her shattered, her thoughts chaotic as they tried to comprehend the raw hunger she had seen in his eyes for one fleeting moment.

Lauren looked at her watch. It was nearly ten o'clock, the scheduled starting time for the council meeting. Leland's presentation was at the top of the agenda.

"Mr. Donovan," she interrupted.

"Yes. What is it, Lauren?"

She pointed to her watch.

"Oh, my. You're right. It is about that time. Well, Lee, are you ready?"

Sighing deeply, he replied, "As ready as I'll ever be. Let's go."

Together they walked upstairs to the large, rectangular council chamber, which was crammed to capacity. As they worked their way through the crowd, Lauren reached out and touched Leland's arm. When he looked down at her, she whispered, "Good luck." He forced a thin smile, then moved on to the seats near the front that had been saved for them.

While they waited for the councilmen to be seated and the onlookers to quiet down, Lauren looked around the room, her eyes coming to rest on a full-length portrait of George Washington. It was just one of the paintings of historical figures in the chamber, and she wondered if the men who sat here now were ever intimidated by their surroundings or if the greatness represented served, instead, to inspire them.

As soon as the meeting was called to order, Lauren could feel her anxiety mounting. Leland sat next to her in stony silence, his face a mask, his muscles taut with tension.

When the mayor announced Leland's building proposal, there was a murmur from the crowd. Most Charleston residents, steeped in Southern manners, were too polite to shout out their anger, but their sentiments were clear from their hostile looks in Leland's direction. Mason Hart was standing at the side of the room, scribbling rapidly in a notebook. Already Lauren could sense the play this story would get in tomorrow's paper.

As soon as the onlookers had quieted down, the mayor proceeded. "Now, if everybody here will just settle down a bit, we can get started. I know you all have some things to say about this office tower, and you'll all get a chance to speak up, but first we've got to get the proposal officially presented to the council.

"Mr. Cross, would you like to proceed, or would you prefer Mr. Donovan to begin?"

"I'll begin, Mr. Mayor," Leland said, taking his artist's renderings and diagrams with him up to a microphone.

"Gentlemen, I'm aware that this proposal has already stirred a great deal of controversy in Charleston. Let me assure you that it was never my intention to plunder this city's waterfront or in any way damage its fine traditions," Leland said, turning to smile at the women from the preservation society. Lauren noticed that almost despite themselves the women warmed to his charm and honesty. They returned the smile.

"A great deal of media time and energy has been devoted to attacking this proposal. That's certainly the right of the various stations and the press. However, I think their call to arms might have been a bit premature, as you will see in just a moment."

Lauren looked at Reed in confusion. "What does he mean? This is no time to be attacking the media."

"Just wait, my dear. You'll see."

In front of her Leland started to lift the drape from the first picture; then he paused and let it drop back into place.

"Before I begin, there are a few more things I would like to explain. What you will see today are not the original plans for the Cross office tower. Nor is my proposal the one discussed initially with the planning and zoning department. However, Mr. Donovan is aware of the changes and has approved them. I'm sure he'll speak to you on that point later."

Again, there was a murmur from the crowd. Lauren was watching Leland closely, her hands clenched tightly in her lap. She couldn't begin to imagine what he was talking about, but she sensed that it was going to make a tremendous difference in the crowd's reactions. She was as eager for him to begin as the rest of the residents were wary. As he lifted the covering from the artist's rendering, there was a gasp of surprise and approval.

Instead of the glass and steel tower originally envisioned, here was a graceful blending of the old and new. At street level and for several floors above, the façade was old brick, trimmed in the wrought ironwork that made so many of the city's buildings distinctive. The higher floors were more modern, but the design worked.

Next he brought out a street map of the area along the waterfront.

"As you know, this tower was originally proposed for this area along here," he said, using a pointer to trace the land along Concord Street. "However, it has been pointed out to me by a number of people that using this particular site would destroy not only some future parkland, but at least two structures of historical significance for the city.

"Therefore," he continued, moving the pointer over several blocks, "I have entered into negotiations for this property here. The sale is contingent on your approval."

Turning back to the women from the preservation group, he winked broadly. "By the way, I have made sure that there is absolutely nothing of historical importance on this block with the possible exception of the dirt. George Washington probably stepped on it. He seemed to be everywhere."

The women laughed with him and the entire crowd broke into enthusiastic applause.

"Gentlemen, I'll be glad to answer any of your questions," he said, when the noise had finally abated.

The next hour was a blur to Lauren. The councilmen questioned Leland closely, then allowed those scheduled to speak to have their say. Most of them, admitting they'd entered the chambers opposed to the tower, said they'd been convinced the new plan would not be a detriment to the city.

"We were afraid this would be the start of Charleston becoming a gloomy, gray jungle," one man said. "Looks to me as though Mr. Cross got our message."

At last the mayor called a halt to the comments from the audience.

"Well, Mr. Cross, I must say you've certainly surprised us all today, but it's been a pleasant surprise. We will have to have another hearing, of course, but I think your proposal looks quite sound. It'll be a great boon to Charleston's future growth."

The meeting then recessed, so the chamber could be cleared of spectators. Lauren gave Reed Donovan a sharp glance. "Why did he do it?" she asked.

"Why don't you ask him that?" he suggested, pushing her toward Leland, who was surrounded by well-wishers and reporters. Lauren stood on the edge of the crowd, listening to his comments, happy that his dream was so close to becoming a reality.

Mason Hart edged his way into the throng.

"Mr. Cross!"

Leland looked around at him. "Yes, Mr. Hart. What can I do for you?"

"Tell me. What made you alter your plans?"

Leland's eyes sought out Lauren.

"Sometimes you have to know when to change, when to fight for something you believe in or when to give up. Some people very dear to me made me realize that a change would benefit everyone in this particular case. I'll save my battles for another war. Now, if you'll excuse me, there's someone I must see."

Lauren practically held her breath as he began making his way toward her. She had recognized the significance of his words and that familiar look in his eyes. Perhaps it was possible for them to work things out after all.

Just then Rod Stevens came up to her.

"Lauren, I've been looking everywhere for you. You're so little, you disappeared in this crush," he said, taking her arm and smiling down at her.

Lauren's greeting was distracted. She tried to look past him to find Leland, but he had turned away from her and was walking stiffly out the door. Seeing him leave, she wanted to shout after him, to stop him. It was as though the very essence of her being, the spark that gave her life was going through that door and she had no way to bring him back.

CHAPTER FOURTEEN

During the next few weeks Lauren felt as though she were caught up in an unending nightmare. Thoroughly bewildered by Leland's abrupt departure from the council chambers on the morning of the public hearing, she lay awake nights going over and over those few moments. She recalled the look of betrayal and then anger that had so quickly replaced the expression of warmth and love she was so sure she had glimpsed. But why that sudden change? She could make no sense of it.

If the long hours until dawn were a torment when she was awake, it was even worse when she dozed off. Her dreams were filled with a relentless barrage of scenes in which a mocking Leland walked away from her and into the waiting arms of Gloria Trudeau. Lauren would wake from these dreams with her heart thundering in her chest and her body bathed in perspiration.

173

"I can't go on like this," she whispered after waking once again from one of those dreams in the grim, lonely hours before sunrise.

It had never been like this after Doug's death, perhaps because that had been so final. There had been nothing she could do to change it. She could only go on. Now there were choices; if only she could make one.

"You made one, you idiot," she mumbled as she sat propped up in bed, her knees drawn up under her chin. "You asked for a divorce."

What puzzled her now was why she was so reluctant to see it through. Surely she had more than enough evidence that the marriage was a dreadful mistake. It had been from the beginning. So why did a tiny part of her, buried deep in her heart, continue to deny that?

"Don't listen to your heart. That's what got you into this mess," she repeatedly reminded herself. And she would almost win the argument until the memories of Leland's touch, of the fire that coursed through her veins at the sight of him, of all those moments of intimacy and loving came flooding back to haunt her. Those memories played havoc with her good intentions.

If only I could talk to him, she thought, but it seemed unlikely she would get the chance. His meetings with Reed had been curtailed now that the office tower proposal was officially before the council. When he had called the office, he had an uncanny knack for placing the calls when she was out to lunch. In class he came late and left hurriedly. When he spoke to her at all, it was with an icy detachment edged in bitterness.

Her pride kept her from seeking him out, especially once the rumors about his romance with a glamorous New York model, Gloria of course, began circulating around town. When the couple's picture appeared on the society page one morning, Lauren's hand shook so badly her coffee spilled from the cup, scalding her arm. She imagined she saw pity in everyone's eyes and it made her more and more reclusive. She spent all her nights home alone with Holly.

Even Holly was being affected by her moods. Not only did she miss Leland herself, but she sensed something of her mother's anguish and tried in her childlike way to be on her best behavior. More and more frequently, though, she was begging to be allowed to go next door to play with David, in an atmosphere free from strain. Lauren realized what was happening, what she was doing to her daughter, and tried to snap out of it, but she could not.

She was home alone one night, staring at the fire as though in a trance, when the doorbell rang. It was Leland.

"You look like hell," he said when she opened the door. His eyes took in her mussed hair, the old bathrobe that hung loosely since she'd lost weight from her already too-thin body.

"Thanks a lot," she said sarcastically. "I needed that."

"Looks to me as though what you need is a good shaking. What are you doing to yourself?"

"Did you come over here to insult me or did you

have another purpose in mind?" she asked, regaining a little of her spirit.

"Actually I came to see Holly. Where is she?"

"She's next door," Lauren said, her listlessness returning. "Go on over. I'm sure she'll be delighted to see you."

"Lauren, look, couldn't we . . ." His voice trailed off.

"Couldn't we what?"

"Nothing. Never mind," he said, his hopelessness seeming to match her own. He walked down the steps, his shoulders slumped. "I'll see you later, Lauren."

"Sure. Later." She watched him go, the feeling of emptiness returning in even more agonizing waves. "Lee, wait," she called out. But it was too late. He'd already gone.

Back inside, Lauren knew she could not spend another evening alone with her depressing thoughts. She called Rod.

"Could you come over, please," she begged, her voice shaky.

"Lauren, what is it? What's wrong?" he asked, his voice filled with concern.

"I . . . I just need someone to talk to. Can you come?"

"I'll be there in a few minutes."

Quickly she showered, put on jeans and a print blouse, and used a light dusting of blusher to disguise her pallor. She had a fresh pot of coffee on the stove by the time Rod arrived.

Sitting at the kitchen table with coffee and a pie that Elsie had brought over, Lauren began to feel a little foolish about her panicked call. Unwilling to discuss the real reasons behind it, she steered the conversation off on a casual, impersonal track. Rod seemed willing to follow her lead.

The young man was such an easy-going, undemanding companion that Lauren soon forgot her problems, thankful to be able to push them aside for a few brief hours. He was telling her about an incident at the diner where some of Leland's students had been going after class.

"This waitress came in, boasting about all her years of experience at the best clubs in Charleston, so Nick, the owner, he hired her. Right away she was in charge of everything, telling everybody what to do. Only trouble was half the time she was rip-roaring drunk.

"Finally one night she goes up to Nick and starts telling him off. She says he should fire the cook. When he refused, she quit and walked off in a rage."

Lauren looked at him expectantly. "So? What's so odd about that?"

Rod grinned. "Nothing. But the next day she turned up in his office again, an application in her hand. She wanted a job."

"What? You're kidding."

"Uh-uh. She was serious. She had no notion she'd ever worked there before."

Lauren laughed so hard, there were tears rolling down her cheeks.

"Oh, Rod. That's incredible!"

"Isn't it?" he agreed, joining in her laughter.

Neither of them heard the front door open or the

sound of Holly calling out. Suddenly she was there in the doorway.

"Mommy, guess what? Lee came to see me," she announced, squealing in her excitement. "See, Mommy. Here he is."

Lauren's laughter died as she looked up to see Leland standing stiffly behind Holly, his eyes disapproving as they moved from her to Rod.

"I brought Holly home. I thought it might be getting close to her bedtime," he said curtly. "I'll be on my way."

"No, please, Mr. Cross," Rod said, jumping to his feet. "I was just about to leave."

Leland waved him back. "Nonsense. There's no need for you to go on my account, Stevens."

His words were bland enough, but the look he gave the two of them was damning. Quickly he brought his outrage under control and turned to pick up Holly.

"Good night, little one. I'll see you again in a few days, okay?"

She gave him a moist kiss on the cheek and clung to him. "Do you have to go, Lee? Can't you stay here again?"

Leland's eyes met Lauren's and a flicker of the old electricity flared between them. For a brief moment they were lost in time, back a few weeks when the heat of their passion had been all that mattered. And then it was over.

"No, baby. I don't think so. I'm sorry."

Quickly he put Holly down and strode from the room without a backward glance. Only the sound of the front door being shut quietly but forcefully shattered the tense silence in the kitchen.

At last Rod spoke. "I think I should go, Lauren."

"No. Don't. Let me get Holly to bed and I'll be right back."

Holly, her tiny back straight, shook her head. "I can put myself to bed, Mommy. I don't need you!"

That final cry as she ran from the room pierced Lauren's heart.

"Wait. Please," she begged Rod as she went after Holly.

Later, they talked far into the night. Rod's mere presence was soothing, but, in the end, nothing had changed. When he left, she was still alone with her broken dreams.

In the morning, though, the memory of Holly's heart-wrenching declaration brought Lauren to a decision. While she might not be able to bring herself to see an attorney and file for divorce, she could, at least, make an effort to end this self-imposed period of mourning. It was significant, she thought, that her decision was being made on Thanksgiving. It was about time she remembered all she had to be thankful for.

Dressing to go to Elsie's for dinner, she took special care with her appearance for the first time in weeks. She picked out a favorite salmon-pink dress that flattered her figure and her coloring. She brushed her hair until it shone, then pulled it back from her face with flowered combs that matched the dress.

"Mommy, you look beautiful," Holly announced after making a careful inspection.

"Thanks, pumpkin. You look pretty special yourself in that red plaid dress. You look just right for Thanksgiving."

"I can hardly wait. Do you suppose we'll have turkey and stuffing at Elsie's?"

"I don't imagine Elsie would dream of offering you anything less, you little gourmet," Lauren said, laughing at Holly's doubtful expression.

"What's a gourmet?"

"Someone who expects only the best food," she replied, brushing on her mascara and taking a final close look at her makeup. "You all set? Have you got the card you made for Elsie and Henry at school?"

"Oh, no-o-o," she moaned. "It's in my room."

"Well, run and get it and we'll be on our way. I want to get over there in time to help with dinner."

Fifteen minutes later, as they pulled into the Cates' driveway, the couple opened the front door to greet them. Holly ran to them and proudly presented them with their card, a picture of a pilgrim she'd drawn in kindergarten.

"Oh, my, isn't this lovely!" Elsie praised her. "I'll just hang this right up in my kitchen where I can see it when I cook.

"How are you, dear?" she called to Lauren, subtly nodding her approval at the improvement in her appearance.

Lauren's improved mood seemed to lift everyone's spirits and the atmosphere was gay as she and Elsie worked side by side preparing the oyster dressing for the plump turkey, peeling the potatoes, and snapping the green beans. In no time the kitchen was filled with delicious aromas.

"Would you like me to set the table now?" Lauren asked.

"No, dear, it's already done. You just sit right here and talk to me while I finish fixing up this cream cheese stuffing for the celery. How's everything down at City Hall these days? I must say I miss it more than I thought I would."

"Don't tell me you're already tired of going fishing with Henry?"

Elsie laughed. "No, indeed. Actually, I've become quite adept at avoiding those outings. It seems I make a bit too much noise for his liking. He thinks I scare away the fish."

"Why Elsie Cates, you old sneak. I'll bet you do that on purpose," Lauren said. "You should be ashamed of yourself."

"Oh, I am. I am," Elsie said, winking broadly and chuckling. Lauren joined in the laughter.

Just then the doorbell chimed and for a fraction of a second Elsie looked flustered. Quickly busying herself at the oven, basting the turkey, she said, "Honey, would you mind getting that? I think Henry's gone up to the attic with Holly."

When Lauren opened the front door and found Leland waiting there, she was speechless. Open-mouthed, she looked helplessly back toward the kitchen, as though willing Elsie to come make this mirage disappear.

"Hello, Lauren," he said, as ill at ease as she was. "I should have known Elsie would do something like this. Would you like me to leave?"

Lauren's heart was pounding so loudly she almost felt she'd need to shout to be heard over its roar.

"No, please. Come in," she said, her voice barely above a whisper. "It's all right."

Leland looked skeptical.

"Are you sure? Don't you think everyone would be more comfortable if I simply left now?"

Although Lauren's hands seemed to be fluttering about nervously with a will of their own, she managed to get her voice under control. "No. Stay. We're adults. Surely we can manage to be civil for one afternoon. It apparently means a lot to Elsie. Couldn't we try?"

His gray eyes locked with hers, their message unreadable. "Sure. Why not?" As they traveled slowly over her body, the corners of his mouth lifted in a trace of a smile. "You're looking much better than you did the last time I saw you."

"Th-thank you," she stammered, a blush rising to add to the rosiness of her cheeks, already warmed by the kitchen's heat.

"The flour's a nice touch too," he teased.

"What?" she asked, lifting her hand to her cheek. But his was there first, gently brushing away the streak of white.

An electric current seemed to charge through Lauren's body. She stood trembling before him as his hand slid tenderly up the side of her face to brush a wisp of a curl back into place. She lifted her eyes to his and read in them the same longing, the same instinctive hunger that was making her pulse throb. She took a tiny, almost imperceptible step toward him and then, with a swiftness that left her gasping for breath, she was in his arms.

Leland groaned as he crushed the full length of her

soft body to his hard leanness. His lips ravished hers in a demanding kiss that tried to make up for weeks of abstinence. Lauren was almost lost to the passion of the moment, her body yielding to his in a total admission of possession. But then there were voices and the sound of footsteps on the stairs. Reluctantly Leland withdrew his arms, leaving Lauren feeling weak and bereft.

Holly caught sight of Leland and cried out gleefully. Henry was beaming as he shook Leland's hand and gave Lauren a knowing look. Elsie, feeling a certain safety in numbers, dared now to come out of the kitchen, hugging Leland warmly and trying to avoid Lauren's eyes. But the fleeting moment of intimacy which had rekindled all the old emotions rendered Lauren incapable of condemning Elsie for her matchmaking.

The afternoon passed in a gloriously happy daze for Lauren. Dinner had been a mouthwatering success, from the crisply browned turkey right on through to the pumpkin pie topped with mounds of whipped cream.

Once the dishes had been cleared away but left for washing later at Elsie's insistence, everyone settled in the living room with the last of the white wine from dinner. Holly had fallen asleep in Leland's lap, a picture of contentment that Lauren wished she could capture forever. Henry caught her wistful expression and, picking up his glass of wine, said, "I think we should have a toast."

Lifting his glass to each of them in turn, he said, "To the past and all the good things it's given us.

And to the future, which promises to be even brighter."

Shyly Lauren looked at Leland as she drank the toast and he reached across the sofa to squeeze her hand. Elsie and Henry watched them and exchanged a conspiratorial wink. It appeared the future would be very bright indeed for these two young people they loved.

CHAPTER FIFTEEN

Minutes later the tranquility of the holiday afternoon with its undercurrents of hope was shattered by the chiming of the doorbell.

"Now, who on earth can that be," Elsie muttered, smoothing her dress and patting her hair into place as she bustled to the door.

The voices in the foyer were muffled for a moment, but then a radiant Gloria Trudeau burst into the room, followed by an agitated Elsie.

"Darling, I'm sorry I couldn't get here any sooner," she announced to Leland, ignoring the look of shock that had registered on his face at her entrance. She brushed his cheek with a kiss before going over to Henry, who was eying her with a look of rising indignation.

"You must be Mr. Cates," she said, extending her hand. "I'm Gloria Trudeau, Lee's friend." The last was said with a soft purr, intended to indicate that their relationship went much deeper then mere friendship.

She barely nodded at Lauren before squeezing in next to her on the sofa, thus separating her from Leland.

Elsie, hoping to smooth over a situation that threatened to explode with tension at any moment, mustered every ounce of her Southern hospitality to offer Gloria a glass of wine.

"Thank you. Wine would be lovely," Gloria said, looking around the room disdainfully. "What a nice little place you have here, Mr. Cates. Of course, it's nothing like the Taylors'."

Her insulting tone was lost on no one. Excluding the others, she placed a possessive hand on Leland's arm and said, "Darling, it really is too bad that you had to miss dinner over there. They are such interesting people. Why, John Taylor has traveled just about everywhere."

"He's also a crashing bore, Gloria," Leland said.

"That may be, darling, but he's a *wealthy* crashing bore and you never know when someone like that might come in handy in your career."

"Gloria, I certainly hope my career will never depend on people like John Taylor. If it does, I'll throw in the towel and spend the rest of my days fishing like Henry here. He's the one who's got his priorities in order."

"Fishing," Gloria repeated, a sneer in her voice. "Darling, I hardly think you're suited for that sort of existence."

"Oh? And why not?" Lauren interrupted, her

voice filled with fury. "Isn't that good enough, Gloria?"

"Lauren," Henry interrupted, trying to stop her.

"No, Henry, I'm not through yet," Lauren said, turning back to Gloria, her eyes flashing with anger. "How dare you come into this home and insult these people! Elsie and Henry Cates have more class than you'll ever have, you . . . you little tramp."

Whirling on Leland, she shouted, "As for you, you're despicable. Inviting this woman here when you knew very well that the Cateses are my friends. With your incredible lack of judgment and her morals, you two deserve each other."

She ran from the room, nearly hysterical.

"I'm sorry," she sobbed, as she passed Elsie and went out into the night, oblivious to the chill in the air.

At the end of the driveway she stumbled and fell, twisting her ankle painfully. Still she refused to go back, instead slowing her pace to limp along, instinctively heading for the solace of White Point Gardens, which was bathed with the shimmering light of the moon.

Finding a bench, she sat down to stare across the still water at the shadow of Fort Sumter. Behind her the mansions of the Battery provided a comforting backdrop. But the familiar setting became a taunting reminder of Gloria's rude remarks as Lauren remembered that the illustrious Taylors lived in one of these houses. Perhaps even now Gloria was back there, Leland at her side.

"Damn her! Damn her!" she muttered. "Who does she think she is, coming into Elsie's home and attacking her and humiliating me? And Lee. My God, what kind of a man is he to allow it? They do deserve each other. They're both vicious, cruel people."

"Are you referring to me," a voice inquired softly as Leland stepped from the shadows to sit next to her on the bench.

"Yes, as a matter of fact, I was," she said defiantly. "Now would you mind getting away from me. I left Elsie's because I couldn't bear your company a moment longer. I still can't."

"That's too bad, because I have no intention of moving from this bench until you and I talk."

"Then I'll leave," she said, hobbling off.

"What in God's name did you do to yourself?" he asked, lifting her off her feet and setting her back on the bench. She tried to slap his hands away, but he ignored her and went right on removing her shoe and examining her swollen ankle.

"How did you do this?" he asked again.

"I fell."

"I figured that much. Where?"

"In the driveway at Elsie's."

"You know, my pet, you really are incredibly stupid sometimes. You walked all this way on it. Don't you know you probably made it worse?"

"It's not that bad," Lauren insisted defensively. "I made it down here, didn't I? I can make it back again."

"We'll see about that. At least maybe it'll force you to sit still for a minute and listen to me," he said, tucking her shoe in his pocket, as though for insurance against her leaving.

"You feel like talking, you talk. I have nothing to say."

"That's just fine. Then I won't have to worry about any interruptions. I have plenty to say."

Suddenly Lauren didn't want to hear any of it—the lies, the excuses. The confusion would just start all over again. Perhaps if she could get him to talk about Gloria all her anger would come flooding back and there would be no danger.

"Where's Gloria?"

"I thought you weren't going to talk. Forget Gloria. She's not important."

Lauren's laugh was harsh. "Have you mentioned that to her?"

"Yes. Several times. But she is one persistent lady and you haven't helped matters by walking out on me. She has this crazy notion that if you're out of my life, I'll marry her."

"And won't you?" Lauren asked, holding her breath as she waited for his reply.

"No, I won't, you little fool! I love you. I've always loved you, ever since that day you knocked me on my head in the street. I think that bump did something to my senses. I haven't had a moment's peace since. Gloria was just . . . just an interlude, like all the others. They meant nothing."

For a moment Lauren thought her heart would burst with joy. Leland loved her, not Gloria! She was almost ready to reach out to him, but the weeks of doubts could not be erased that easily. There was more that she had to know.

"She said . . . she said you were with her after we got married."

189

"With her?" Leland's look was puzzled at first, then incredulous. He started laughing.

"It's not funny. Were you with her?" Lauren insisted.

"I had dinner with her, if that's what you mean."

"You know it's not."

"No, Lauren," he said, his tone sobering. "There was nothing more between Gloria and me after our wedding. God knows I had plenty of reason to turn to another woman. You, my own wife, had walked out on me the day after the wedding. When I got back here you kept me at arm's distance, almost as though you couldn't stand the sight of me. And then, then you demand a divorce because you're in love with another man. Oh, yes, my dear, I had plenty of reason to turn to Gloria."

His voice had risen to an angry pitch, but he lowered it as he looked Lauren directly in the eyes. "But I didn't sleep with her, Lauren."

Lauren heard the bitterness in his voice and his charge about another man with a feeling of shock. "Another man? Lee, there is no other man. There never has been."

"What about Rod Stevens? Every time I turned around there he was, laughing with you, touching you. It nearly drove me mad."

"Rod?" Lauren's voice was choked with barely controlled laughter. "Darling, Rod is a friend, a very dear friend who's been trying to hold me together ever since I thought I'd lost you."

Leland's face reflected his confusion. "But when you told me to get the divorce, you said there were grounds—adultery."

190

Suddenly Lauren could hold back the laughter no longer, as relief washed over her.

"Oh, darling, don't you see? I thought you were the one who'd provided the grounds. With Gloria."

Then she was in his arms and he was wiping away the tears of joy, his kisses trailing along her neck to seek the soft hollow at its base. With a shudder he brought his lips down on hers, devouring her mouth, his tongue making an impassioned assault on the sensitive skin inside. His hands, firm and demanding, stroked and massaged until her body radiated a fiery heat that began deep in the core of her being. She molded herself to him, wanting to feel the closeness she had desired for weeks now.

He pulled her onto his lap, his hands slipping through the opening in the front of her dress to tease and tantalize the rosy peaks of her breasts into hardened pebbles of sensitivity. Each touch brought her closer to the edge of a precipice, one she didn't want to go over alone. Her breathing ragged and uneven, she pulled back from his embrace to protest.

"Oh, no, you don't," he whispered hoarsely, holding her tightly and continuing his merciless pattern of stroking, lifting her senses to delirious heights.

"Oh, Lee, I love you so much," she cried out at last, clinging to him as though he might disappear. Never again would she be afraid of his ability to stir her, to possess her so completely.

Lauren was sure now of his love and it filled her with a radiant feeling of happiness.

Her eyes dark pools of fulfillment, she whispered, "Darling, let's go home."

"Sure you wouldn't rather hobble back to Elsie's by yourself," he asked lightly.

"Not a chance," she said huskily, kissing him deeply again.

"Then home it is," he said when he could speak again. "Tonight and always."